D1360437

the Sisters club

Megan McDonald

American Girl

SCHOLASTIC INC.

New York Toronto London Auckland Sydney
Mexico City New Delhi Hong Kong Buenos Aires

No part of this publication may be reproduced, stored in a retrieval system, or transmitted in any form or by any means, electronic, mechanical, photocopying, recording, or otherwise, without written permission of the publisher. For information regarding permission, write to Pleasant Company Publications, 8400 Fairway Place, P.O. Box 620998, Middleton, WI 53562.

ISBN 0-439-83457-0

Text copyright © 2003 by Megan McDonald. Cover and some interior illustrations copyright © 2003 by Pleasant Company. Some interior illustrations copyright © 2003 by Linda Ketelhut. Special thanks to Eliza Broaddus for the poem "I'm Sorry" on page 90. All rights reserved. Published by Scholastic Inc., 557 Broadway, New York, NY 10012, by arrangement with Pleasant Company Publications. SCHOLASTIC and associated logos are trademarks and/or registered trademarks of Scholastic Inc.

12 11 10 9 8 7 6 5 4 3 2 1   5 6 7 8 9 10/0

Printed in the U.S.A.   40

First Scholastic printing, November 2005

American Girl® is a registered trademark of Pleasant Company. Interior illustrations by Linda Ketelhut and Leslie Cober-Gentry. "This Is Just to Say" by William Carlos Williams, from COLLECTED POEMS: 1909–1939, VOLUME 1, copyright © 1938 by New Directions Publishing Corp. Reprinted by permission of New Directions Publishing Corp.

For my sisters,
Susan, Deborah, Michele, and Melissa

Table of Contents

ACT ONE

Stevie

The Sisters Club was my (brilliant!) idea. Sisters only. Just the three of us—Alex, the oldest of the Reel family sisters; Joey, the youngest; and me (Stevie) in the middle. That's the way it was, is, and always will be, forever and ever. Amen.

My best friend-who's-not-a-sister, Olivia, was licking all the pink icing off a mashed-in cupcake after school one day. She just didn't get The Sisters Club.

"Stevie, how can it be a club if it's just made up of people in your own family, and nobody else can join?"

"I'm sorry. It just is," I told her. She stuck out her pink-icing tongue at me. "Anything can be a club. Give me some of that." I stole some of her icing. "See? Now you and me are in The Pink Icing Club."

"But you're already sisters," said Olivia. "Why do you need a special club?"

"Because."

"C'mon. What's the big deal? Just make

me an honorary sister, so I can be in the club. Reel sister number four—Olivia Duncan Reel. See? It sounds like an actor, you have to admit."

"Oh no, not you, too," I said. "My whole family is cuckoo about acting—except me."

"Three people never works, you know," Olivia told me.

"How come? I mean, look, it had to work in this family, ever since Joey got born."

"Think about it. One person always gets left out. Take the Three Stooges. Everybody knows Curly and Moe. Like when they're stuck in that cow costume and the other one tries to milk them? But who's the other one?"

"Stooge Number Three," I said.

"Or, or, or . . . the Three Musketeers," Olivia said.

"Nobody knows any of the Musketeers! I think you've been watching the old-movie channel too much," I said.

"I'm telling you, one always gets left out.

Or somebody gets tired of it, or gets her feelings hurt. Or somebody gets mad at somebody else. And you won't like it when it happens. Trust me," Olivia said.

"Fine by me, as long as the one who gets left out is Joey." I cracked up.

"You'll see."

Olivia has to be wrong. That's the thing about sisters. Mom always says it—sisters are there for you forever. "You'll always have your sisters, no matter what." But I can't help feeling funny, somewhere deep down in a teeny, tiny part of me. What if it happens to us? What if I'm the one who gets left out or something?

I tell myself, *it's different with sisters.*

In The Sisters Club, we have a charter and everything. At least that's what Alex calls it. Joey didn't know what a charter was (I thought it was a boat, but don't tell) until Alex told her, "It's like the Constitution."

Joey was thrilled.

"It sounds so important!" she said, and right away she started drawing us our own Sisters Club flag.

Me, I think of it like a secret pact. Something that holds us together.

At one of our SCMs (Sisters Club Meetings), Alex was wearing a witch's hat and saying "Double, double, toil and trouble" into the mirror when we made up our own saying for The Sisters Club. Alex asked, "What rhymes with sisters?" and Joey said, "Blisters!" Then I said, "Sisters, blisters. It sounds like a tongue twister."

Voila! We came up with our very own chant:

Sisters, blisters, and tongue twisters!

Now we say it first off whenever we have The Sisters Club.

Alex makes a lot of the rules, and Joey writes them down in her notebook. Alex keeps making up new rules all the time, so Joey has to keep adding stuff to her notebook all the time.

The Sisters Club Charter
by Joey Reel

Clubhouse: Alex's room

Members: Reel sisters only

Uniform: PJ's are good. Plaid is bad (according to Fashion Queen Alex), except when it's PJ's.

Mascot: Alex's sock monkey, named Sock Monkey (I wish it was Hedgie, my hedgehog.)

Logo: Three sock monkeys holding pinkies

Alternate logo: Troll doll with the "no" sign over it (red circle with slash through middle)

Secret handshake: Hook pinkies together while saying, "Sisters, blisters, and tongue twisters"

Secret knock: I don't know how to write it! I just know how to do it. Sounds like Da da da, da dee dee doh

Password: Shakespeare (Alex
thought it up. Shh! Don't tell!)
Activities: Tell secrets and scary
stories, eat popcorn and ice cream,
stay up late, have sleepovers in
Alex's room (I mean, the clubhouse!)
Dues: Only if we need popcorn or
ice cream and we're out
Rules: No throwing pillows or other
   objects, except in an official
   pillow fight
   No using Alex's brush to brush
   your hair
   No taking anything from Alex's
   room (especially anything with
   glitter)
   No saying "nut job" or "nut
   ball" (it bugs Alex)

Cartoon by Stevie

Joey and I go to Alex's room. My sister's lying across her bed with her head dangling upside down, off the other side.

This is either:
a beauty secret
a brain boost
a way to check for scary spiders on
   the ceiling

Stevie

"No saying 'nut job'" is Alex's latest rule, which Joey has added to the list. Of course Joey has to ask, "What's a nut job?"

"It's a peanut that's looking for work," Alex says. The two of us crack up.

"OK, I have a rule," says Joey. "No doing that."

"What?"

"That thing where you don't answer a question right. Then you laugh and act like I'm a nut job."

"No saying 'nut job'!" screams Alex.

All three of us pile on the bed, laughing our heads off.

"But can we at least say 'nut' or 'job,' even if we don't say them together?"

"NO!" screams Alex again. "Because that would make you a nut job."

We die laughing some more, which Joey says is the best part of The Sisters Club.

For me, the best part has always been the Remembering Game. Alex is the best at it.

Alex

Players: Three sisters
Setting: Joey and Stevie are in my room bugging me again.

Joey: Sisters, blisters, and tongue twisters. Let's play the Remembering Game!

Alex: Do you both solemnly swear not to repeat anything you're about to hear?

Stevie and Joey: We do!

Alex: OK, everybody pull up a pillow. (We all lie on pillows and stare up at the ceiling.)

Joey: Tell one about me!

Alex: Joey, remember when you were a snowflake in first grade and you couldn't fit through the door?

Joey: Yeah! I got stuck trying to get into my class, so I had to walk sideways, and I poked Matthew Malin with one of my six points.

Stevie: And your teacher tried to tell him it was snowing to make him feel better.

Joey: He still doesn't like me!

Stevie: No wonder.

Alex: Stevie, remember that time you wore your pajama top to school by mistake?

Stevie: It was pajama day!

Alex: Was not! OK, then, remember when you stole that blue marble from the Ben Franklin store, and—

Joey: What? You <u>stole</u>?

Alex: Don't worry. Stevie felt so bad, she went and turned herself in. All they did was make her put it back.

Stevie: My turn. Remember when Joey begged Mom and Dad to let her see the elephants at the zoo, and then, when she saw them, she threw up?

Alex: That's the best!

Joey: How come all the throwing-up stories are about me?

Alex: They just are. We never throw up. OK, I have one about me. How about the time I convinced you to put marshmallows between your toes?

Joey: I don't remember that.

Alex: Good. Because we haven't done it yet. We're going to do it right now.

Stevie: No way am I putting marshmallows in between my toes.

Joey: Toe jam!

Alex: It's a new beauty tip. Helps make your skin softer, AND it makes it easier to paint your toenails! I read it in a magazine.

Joey: Glitter toenails—cool!

Stevie: Like I really care about toenails. And just one time I'd like to see one of these famous magazines you're always quoting.

Alex: Check my locker. They're there.

Stevie: You just say it's in a magazine to make it sound important.

Joey: C'mon, Stevie. It sounds like fun. And we can remember it later!

Stevie: What about The Sisters Club? Marshmallow feet are not in the charter. There are rules!

Alex: New rule. Joey, write this down. All members of The Sisters Club must try putting marshmallows between their toes if they want to be in the club.

Joey's Homework Notebook

I have this notebook. It looks like a real one for school. Actually, I pretend like it's a diary, because both of my big sisters, Alex and Stevie, think diaries (especially locked ones!) are way cool.

Hey, I just thought of one thing they agree on!

But really this is going to be my SHN—Secret Homework Notebook. My big sisters think I'm nuts. (#2 thing they agree on!) They hate homework.

But I mean, by third grade, shouldn't a person be old enough to get homework?

All we get are worksheets.

Baby stuff.

So ... I like to make up homework for myself.

Story of My Life
by Joey Reel

My (made-up) homework today is to write about me. Stevie says that's an autobiography. (Ok, she had to help me spell that.) Whatever.

Hi. My name is Joey. Not Joan. Not Jo-Ann or Josephine or Jolene. Not Jo-Anything.

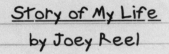

Just Joey.

I guess it's better than Jethro. Or Jerome.

Mom and Dad named us all for boys. For some strange reason, they could only think of good boy names when we were born.

Stevie says Dad wanted a boy. Mom says all three times she was sure she was having a boy. When it got to me, she was really, really, really sure, 'cause boys kick a lot or something.

Even the doctor yelled, "It's a boy!" when I first came out.

But it wasn't a boy! It was me, Joey. And I don't kick, even though Stevie says I do—like when we have sleepovers in Alex's room. But who wouldn't kick in a sleeping bag!

My big sisters call me Duck. See, when I was little, I called everybody (Stevie and Alex) and everything "duck" (the table, our dog, my shoe). Most times I hate being called Duck. It's not like I have two almost-webbed toes (like Stevie!) or anything. It just makes me feel like a baby.

I'm not a baby, no matter what they say.

I read chapter books!

Stevie

Everything about this family is acting, acting, acting. Even the name of our town is Acton, like Act On. We live right next door to the Raven Theater, and my mom, dad, and Alex are all actors.

My dad doesn't act on stage much anymore. He's the set builder for the Raven, so he's always making stuff for this play or that.

Our dining room has been an underground rabbit hole, a Kansas tornado, a Civil War battlefield, a fire station, and a medieval castle where you have to cross a moat just to eat at the table.

Backstage at the Raven is filled with cool stuff everywhere. There are racks of glittery costumes, trunks of weird hats and masks, strange instruments, a forest of cardboard trees, old lamps and chairs, and a papier-mâché dog that Act Two (our dog) likes to bark at. There's even a punched-through door from a play where somebody pretended to get real mad.

People even think our house is a movie set or something. You can be baking cookies with cookie dough smeared on your face or lying on the couch in your pajamas with really bad bed-hair, and strangers press their noses right up to our windows and look in!

I feel like I live in a fishbowl.

If they knew it made their noses look a hundred times bigger, I don't think they'd keep doing it. Of course, when those people look in our window, they might actually see a play sometime.

Dad says, "All the world's a stage, even the living room!"

So he lets us put on *King Lear* in our own living room any time we want.

I never used to want to. I tried telling Dad once. I told him I didn't even like plays. I was missing the Reel acting gene.

"Hogwash!" (He actually said that.) "Everybody likes a good story. Just because you don't go in front of people doesn't mean you don't have an actor in you."

Dad says my star's plenty bright to see

where I'm going. But I'll stick to being a star in the living room, thank you very much.

That's why *King Lear* is the only play I like. And it's about three sisters.

King Lear is Dad's favorite play, too. I wonder why. It's about this guy who has three daughters! They have weird names.

If you think Stevie's a funny name for a girl, try Goneril, Regan, or Cordelia. Cordelia's not so bad. (That's Joey, the youngest, and the good one—King Lear's favorite. Joey never lets me be Cordelia. Not once!) At least Cordelia sounds like a flower, not a yucky disease or a president.

The play is a tragedy. It's supposed to make you cry, but it doesn't. It usually makes us laugh our heads off. (No heads really come off—just eyeballs!) Or we end up in a fight. King Lear (Dad) yells a lot at his daughters (especially the oldest one—Alex. Ha!).

King Lear Props

Map of England (you can write on cloth if you want)
Jester hat (with bells!)
Plastic dagger
Eyeballs! (one guy gets his eyes poked out—gross!)
Cookie sheet (my idea—for making thunderstorm noises!)

Favorite Parts from King Lear

Out, vile jelly
You stinkard
A pox on all this
Off with his head (we say this even if it's not in the play!)
Out with his eyes
Jellied eel and rotten oranges
Roast rat!

The play is about how King Lear gives away his kingdom to his three daughters. Sounds simple, right?

WRONG!

Goneril (Alex) is greedy. Regan (me) says she loves her dad more than Goneril, but she's only pretending. And Cordelia (Joey) really loves him, but she gets kicked out of the kingdom (good move!).

So it seems like the evil sisters win. BUT this guy (Mom—she plays all the other parts, even boys) who likes Joey, I mean Cordelia, pretends to be King Lear's servant and spies on the evil sisters.

King Lear starts to figure out the older ones are evil (I could have told him that!). They each keep pretending the other one is trying to murder King Lear, and they try to poison each other (YES!). People get stabbed (the dagger) and eyeballs come out (POP!).

So King Lear goes outside and yells at a thunderstorm (the cookie sheet!).

He gets to say lots of funny-sounding words like "Alack" and "O nuncle!" and

stuff. I think it's in a big important speech.
I forget.

The sad part is Cordelia dies in the end.
(Who cares—it's just Joey!)

But Dad usually lets her live and get the
kingdom, which makes Alex and me mad.
Then we say how come Joey always gets her
way (so true, even though Joey says it's so
NOT true) and we quit.

The end.

Report on William Shakespeare
by Joey Reel

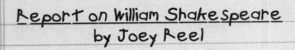

Shakespeare is gross! I don't
  get why Dad likes him so much.
1. In his plays, they throw rats
  and eat eels.
2. They send each other bloody
  napkins.
3. Their brains come out and
  stuff.
4. Number of times Shakespeare
  uses the word "rat" in
  King Lear: 27!
How did a guy who talks so funny
  get way famous? The guy
  says everything backward.
  Go figure.
"I am in love" = "In love I am."
"I will go" = "Go will I."
This is the end.
The end this is.

Alex

I come from a family of actors. Not just Mom and Dad, but a long line.

I love love love living in Acton, because we have a one-hundred-year-old theater and this town has had plays 4ever (as Joey would say).

It all started with our great-great-grandmother, Hepzibiah McNutty. Yep, that's really her name.

When I star in a play, people say, "That's Hezzy's girl," like she's my real, alive grandma living down the street or something, even though she'd be like a million years old.

Stevie says how can I be happy about being descended from anybody named Hepzibiah? She thinks our whole family is Mc-Nutty!

I think old Hezzy is cool. They say she rode a horse for thirteen hours through so much snow that her shoes froze right to the stirrups. Bugs and bears and stuff didn't stop her. But the coolest thing? She wore bloomers and everything, so she could look like a lady but ride horses like a man.

Hey, maybe that's where I get my fashion sense!

Acton wasn't anything but a wide spot in the road back then, so Hezzy built the Raven Theater and put on plays just to give people around here something to do.

Mom wants a real house someday, which means a new one. But this house has history. I mean, Hezzy's ghost could be hanging around in the rafters with the spiderwebs, watching over me. I like thinking Hezzy might have looked out the same window as me, practicing lines for a play.

We still have a cracked hand mirror and some old lace gloves that supposedly belonged to her. Stevie says a cracked mirror is bad luck and we should have sold it for tons of money a long time ago. Then we'd be rich and not living with so many spiders. But I think it's great that acting goes back way way way way way long ago in this family.

How could I not love acting, right? As Dad says, "You're a Reel. It's in the blood."

Stevie

If you are not into acting and theater and plays, do not move to Acton, Oregon. And look out if you are related to some batty old lady named Hepzibiah McNutty. It will drive you nutso. (I did not say "nut job," Alex!) Everybody (mostly pioneer-crazy Joey) acts like it's a really big deal that she came over on the Oregon Trail, but as far as I can tell, she just rode in a wagon and made everybody else do all the work. (Like somebody else I know—Alex!) What kind of a pioneer is that?

I was onstage once, and only once.

I was a Human Piñata. No lie. I did not make this up. I am not exaggerating.

It was my first (and last!) time onstage.

Ask Joey. Ask Alex. Ask half the town of Acton. It was for Joey's birthday one time. Alex convinced me it would be fun to put on a play, and I wanted to be like my big sister, my mom, and my dad. But she did not tell me what the part was.

All I knew was I only had to remember one line. "Yum! Candy!" I knew I could do that. For days, I'd walk around the house reciting, "Yum! Candy!" and rubbing my tummy like I was in a Campbell's Soup commercial or something.

What I didn't know was that I had to dress like Big Bird, get poked with a broomstick, and hang like a beehive in the wind.

The play was about this old washerwoman (Alex, of course) who comes into this house at night. She sees a piñata hanging there, waiting for the birthday party the next day. She knows the piñata is full of candy, and she can't resist trying some. So she gives the piñata—a.k.a. (also known as) me—a poke with her broom!

Dad strapped me into this contraption thingy, which looked like a swing. It had all these straps so I could hang from the beamport, a big opening in the ceiling of the theater where more lights can hang.

It was so hot inside that bird suit, I could hardly breathe. I was pretty much gasping for air. And I remember hearing the little kids in the audience say, "Hey, I hear the piñata breathing!"

Anyway, whenever the washerwoman poked me, no candy was supposed to come out. But when she wasn't looking, I was supposed to say "Yum! Candy!" and throw down some candy to the kids.

That part was fun! At first.

But as soon as the kids started figuring out there was candy in my suit, they all ran up on stage and started jumping at me. They took Alex's broom, and she didn't even try to take it back! I threw down all the candy I had, but they kept poking me to try to get more. By this time, I was spinning around and around in circles. I was so dizzy, I could not feel my head. I was sure I'd throw up.

I yelled, "Stop! Let me down! Hey! Stop!" but the kids just kept jabbing and poking. Dad was operating the ropes from above. When he figured out what was going on, he tried to pull me up instead of lowering me into the sugar-crazed mob. The grand finale:

my Big Bird costume got stuck going through the ceiling.

So, as you can see, being a Human Piñata was not exactly my ticket to stardom. See why I'm not in plays like the rest of the nuts (McNuts!) around here?

Pioneers Rock!
by Joey Reel

The best thing about our town is The Rock, right in the middle of the town square. Dad says it sounds like a jail. Alex says it sounds like a funny nickname for an actor. Mom says it sounds like a big fat diamond ring.

Stevie says it sounds like a rock.

It is! A real rock! Made out of... rock!

I call it Pioneer Rock. It's been there forever, since olden days. Pioneers carved their names there. You can still see "Hepzibiah McNutty" if you know where to look. I've traced over it like gazillions of times. Some rubbings I made are hanging all over one wall of our room.

Stevie says you can almost hear

the wagons creaking and squeaking down the ruts in the road. I think she's just saying it to tease me, but for real you can almost hear it.

If you close your eyes.

They paint the rock now, to tell you when there's a dance, or a play, or a puppet show at the library. Hello! They should not, I repeat, NOT, paint over pioneer names. Pioneers rule!

Mom made a pioneer costume when Alex was little, and she passed it down to Stevie and then Stevie passed it to me. It has a calico dress and apron and a big bonnet and even button-up shoes. I can't wait to wear it for Pioneer Day at school.

Alex and Stevie say it makes me look like a geek. But I think I look like L IW (Laura Ingalls Wilder) and Laura Ingalls Wilder was not a geek! They didn't even HAVE geeks back then.

For Pioneer Day, we get to dry up old apples and make dolls out of them and learn how to churn butter.
Homework to myself: Save old apples.

Joey's favorite stuffed animals

Hedgie (hedgehog with purple hat)
JoJo (penguin)
Pengie (other penguin)
Lucky Bear
Nicky Bear
Sticky Bear
Sugar (used to be Mommy Rabbit)
Somersault Joey
Somersault Stevie (I won it at the fair and gave it to her)
Duck slippers

Stevie

I guess I can see why some crazy old lady stopped her wagon when she got here. Take one look at the mountains and you'd never want to leave, either.

The best view is from a window right in our shower. No lie. When you get up in the morning and look out, the first things you see are the Cascades, with three snow-capped peaks. They're really volcanoes, called the Three Sisters, just like Alex, me, and Joey.

South Sister is the youngest one, like Joey. It's only twenty-five thousand years old. Then there's Middle Sister (me, of course). And North Sister reminds me of Alex. You never know when she's going to erupt (the sister, not the volcano!). There's always something brewing just below the surface, making it interesting.

So I'm taking a shower and there are the mountains looking all picture-postcardy, like you could just lick a stamp and send that view to somebody you love. Early in the morning, when the sun hits just right, the snow looks like it just put on some blush, and in the evening lots of times it looks eerie blue, like how I picture Antarctica.

Blue snow.

It sure gets a person dreaming.

That's pretty much when Alex starts kicking in the bathroom door telling me I take the longest showers in the history of History.

Hey, can I help it if there's a window in the shower?

Mom wants to get a "real" house someday. I do, too—a house where I wouldn't have to have penguins on one-half of the wallpaper (Joey's side) or any wallpaper at all to cover up the hundred-year-old cracks. A house with a room of my own, where I wouldn't have to share a closet or look at names of dead pioneers on the wall or hear Joey say "good night" to like about a hundred fifty stuffed animals every night.

And I could keep the light on as long as I wanted.

But I sure would miss that view.

ACT TWO

Alex

Alex: OK. Are you ready for this? You're never gonna believe what I just heard.

Joey: What? WHAT?

Stevie: You forgot to say "Sisters, blisters, and tongue twisters."

Alex: Joey, maybe you should leave the room. I'm not sure I should say it in front of you.

Joey: No fair! Say it! I'm not a baby!

Alex: (dramatic pause) I heard Mom say she's moving.

Stevie: What? What do you mean, moving?

Alex: As in moving OUT.

Joey: Huh?

Stevie: You're crazy.

Alex: It happens, you know.

Stevie: What happens?

Alex: Divorce! Lots of people get divorces, you know. Over half the kids in my class—

Joey: (holding hands over ears) You're scaring me.

Stevie: What do you mean? Mom and Dad hardly ever even fight.

Joey: (still holding hands over ears) La la la la la—

Alex: Duck! Stop singing. This is serious.

Stevie: Everything with you is serious. You don't even know what you're talking about.

Alex: Oh yeah? I was looking over my piano stuff, and Mom and Dad were in the kitchen, and they didn't even know I was right there in the next room.

Stevie: So?

Alex: Then I heard them talking real low, like they didn't want anybody to hear.

Joey: Maybe they were telling a secret. Did you ever think of that?

Alex: Get real. I'm not kidding. First Dad said, "Are you sure this is what you want?"

Then Mom said, "I have to get out of here— this house. The time has come."

Then Dad said, "As long as you're sure. . . We'll have to tell the girls. This is going to mean a big change for them."

Stevie: You don't know. That could mean anything. Maybe Mom is taking a trip to see her sisters or something.

Alex: A trip is not a BIG CHANGE for us. I'm telling you. You didn't hear it.

Stevie: A pox on all this! Joey, don't listen to her.

Joey: I'm not!

Alex: You'll see!

Stevie

One minute it was just an ordinary
Thursday in the Reel family. The next
minute, Mom dropped the big one on us. It
happened at dinner that night. Not like Alex
said, though. I'm not talking about the big D.
Nope, nothing like divorce or anything.

First of all, I have to tell you about The
Hat. We're talking really embarrassing. See,
there's this jester hat my Dad wore when he
played King Lear for real. It looks kind of
like a droopy crown with bells on the ends.
When somebody has something important
to say in our family, they have to put on The
Hat and announce it like they're the town
crier or something.

Me, I'd rather leave a sticky note on the
fridge.

So, on Thursday, Mom put on The Hat at
dinner.

"Da da–da da!" my dad crowed, like he
was a human trumpet.

"I have some news," Mom started.

"Good news or bad news?" asked Alex. Joey sat up straighter.

"Good news! I'm going back to work. A real acting job. No more bit parts at the Raven. This is my big break. Are you ready for this?"

Mom whipped out a dopey-looking apron that said FONDUE SUE in big fat letters with rolling pins flying around in the background.

"Your name's not Sue," said Joey.

"I'm going to be on TV!" said Mom. "I got my own cooking show. This is my character, Fondue Sue."

"How is this possible?" asked Alex. "You can't even cook!"

"What do you mean? I cook for this family almost every night, in case you haven't noticed," said Mom.

"Yeah, potatoes from a box and spaghetti from a can," Alex said. "They'll have to call your show 'The Art of Opening a Can!'"

Root beer went up my nose. I had to duck to avoid Joey's mashed-potato-from-a-box spray all the way across the table.

"Girls, c'mon now," Dad said. "Let's try to be supportive. This is a big opportunity for Mom."

"Mom, you know what fondue is, right?" Know-It-All Alex asked Mom. "Cheese glop! *Fondue* is French for cheese glop."

"Mom. Name the five food groups," said Little Miss Homework (Joey.)

"Meats, vegetables, fruits. Let me see . . . pretzels and things like that go at the top, right? Junk food?"

"Mo-om. Pretzels are not a food group! They call it 'fats, oils, and sweets,' not 'junk food.' They teach us that in third grade. At the *beginning* of the year."

"Look, they're going to give me all the ingredients," said Mom. "I won't even have to chop a single toe of garlic or sift my own flour. All I have to do is smile and point and read the prompts. Maybe a little stirring and mixing. How hard could it be?"

"Witches stir and mix things," said Joey. "Why don't you just be a witch?"

"Hey, I know! You could be a TV anchorwoman on the eleven-o'clock news!" said Alex. "Or a meteorologist. They smile and point. And you'd get to wear a matching two-piece suit, not a dopey apron with a funny fondue name."

"But I'll be acting," Mom said. "I don't have to know how to cook. That's what acting is."

Mom took off The Hat and set it on the table, all crumply-like.

"This is my chance to make some real money. We could save for a house, a real house of our own, not this cricketty old monster with the falling-down roof."

"We don't have crickets," Joey said. "Or monsters."

"And we're used to the saggy old roof," Alex said. "It's like it's leaning down to hug us. The crooked old floors remember our footsteps—nobody else's. Me: Shiny tap shoes when I was five. Stevie: Flip-flops all year long. Joey: Duck slippers from when she was little."

So what did I do? What I always do: I rushed in to save the day. "It'll be great, Mom. Don't worry. I can cook stuff. Alex and Joey will help me—right, you guys?" Nobody answered.

"Just think," said Alex, "you'll be like that weird lady on the old *Mary Tyler Moore* reruns—the one with the cooking show. She was always making flambé and flan and Florentine stuff. What was her name—Sue Ann?"

"Sue Ann Fondue?" Joey and I sprayed each other with laughter. And more mashed potatoes.

"Say it, don't spray it," said Alex, which made us crack up and spray all the more.

"Sheesh," said Mom. "This cooking thing is going to be a lot more complicated than I thought."

Stevie

See what I mean? You wake up, you brush your teeth, you look out your shower window, you go to school . . . then suddenly everything's upside down. I should have known the Reel family was in big trouble as soon as I saw *The Joy of Cooking*.

It was the very next day after Martha-Stewart-Mom made her big announcement. She hauled this giant book out of the back of a cupboard we use like once a year since you can only reach it by standing on a chair. The book was covered in dust that dated back to the Titanic. Mom dusted it off and cracked open the spine.

"When did you get that?" I asked her, in between choking on one-hundred-year-old dust particles.

"It was a gift, when your dad and I got married."

"Is it an antique?" asked Joey.

"It looks brand-new," I said. (Minus the Titanic dust, that is.)

"I wonder why," said Alex.

"Ha, ha," said Mom, not laughing.

"I thought you were acting," said Alex. "I thought you didn't have to know how to cook."

"Well, I should know something about it," said Mom. "I have to get into my role, after all."

There was no stopping her.

For seven days, we ate Mom's cooking. Whatever she dished up, we ate. Each night's meal was more disgusting than the last.

"What *is* this stuff, anyway?" I couldn't help asking that first night.

"Beef tournedos," said Mom.

"I know why they call it 'tornado,'" said Joey. She pointed to the kitchen, cracking up. It did look like a disaster area.

"Beef tornado! You know I don't eat meat!" Alex said.

"The Queen of Broccoli has spoken!" That was me.

All week, there were quick potato dumplings that needed dumping and cheese puffs that didn't puff. There was chicken à la king without any king and eggs Benedict that even Benedict Arnold would not have tried to eat.

By the fifth night of cooking, Mom stared at the cheese–puff–stained cover of the cookbook. "I don't know why they call this *The Joy of Cooking*," said Mom. Joey and I made eyes at each other. Mom looked at the author of the cookbook. "Who is this Irma S. Rombauer person, anyway? She is going to hear from me."

This is Mom's favorite saying. Whenever she doesn't like something, somebody is going to hear from her.

"I think Irma S. Rombauer is dead, Mom," I said, "on account of the book being like a hundred years old." I opened the book to a random page, looking to prove my point. "Potted goose," I read aloud. "Did they have potted goose in colonial times, when this book was written?" I flipped some more pages. "Marinated wild birds."

"Marinated wild birds!" Alex shouted.

"What kind of person would marinate wild birds? We should throw the book away this second, before the Sierra Club arrests us."

By the end of the week, we were getting desperate—and hungry.

"I know," Joey said, trying to be helpful. "Why don't you make something we've actually heard of? Like Jell-O. You make really good Jell-O."

Joey could live on Jell-O. I'm surprised she doesn't turn into the stuff.

"Ya know," I said, "one day we're gonna wake up and there's gonna be a jiggly mass of green stuff in your bed instead of you. Invasion of the Jell-O monsters."

Joey grinned—like she thought turning into Jell-O was a good idea.

"How about tuna noodle casserole?" I suggested. "It's easy. Everybody knows how to make tuna noodle casserole. You can't go wrong. Look, it says right here in *The No-Joy of Cooking,* page 529, 'excellent emergency dish.'"

"This *is* an emergency," said Mom.

"And if anything goes wrong, I can always put out the fire," Dad called from the hallway. "I played a firefighter back in summer stock one year, remember?"

"Very funny," Mom said. "I'm going to do this, and it's not going to burn. Do you think maybe something's wrong with our oven?"

"As in never been used?" I asked.

"Oh, I see," said Mom. "A whole family of comedians. Too bad they didn't ask me to do stand-up."

That night, Mom minced and whipped and greased and poured and sprinkled and sifted until she had herself one foolproof emergency tuna noodle casserole.

"This is good noodle casserole," Alex said, trying to sound encouraging. "Do you think they make noodle casserole on TV?"

"Not without tuna. I didn't get any tuna in mine," said Joey. I kicked her under the table. "Hey, Stevie kicked me."

"Girls," said Dad.

"I forgot the tuna?" wailed Mom. "I forgot the tuna, didn't I? You can't have tuna noodle casserole without the tuna!"

"It's fine," said Dad. "Yum." For an actor, he wasn't very convincing.

Mom ran to call one of her sisters long-distance, like she always does when things are looking worse than hopeless.

"I think I lost five pounds this week," Alex whispered to me.

"I miss potatoes from a box," I said.

"I miss Mom," said Joey.

My Favorite Dessert
Joey Reel

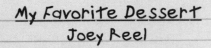

Jell-O is my favorite dessert. It comes in colors. I like the way it wiggles and jiggles and looks like brains. Writing this report made me wonder, what is Jell-O really? I mean, what's it made of?

So I looked it up.
GROSS!

Jell-O is really gelatin, which is really made from animal parts like skin and bones and inside stuff. Bluck!

It's used in foods and film! Double bluck!

I eat film! (But it tastes good.) (Note to self: Don't tell my vegetarian sister Alex. Or do!)

In closing, I would like to say that Jell-O is one of the only things

my Mom makes that I actually like.
When I'm sick, she always makes lime
Jell-O and it helps me feel better.
I hope I never get sick anymore,
because who is going to make me lime
Jell-O?

Little-known facts about Jell-O

Jell-O is over a hundred years old
(older than my Mom's cookbook!).
413,997,403 packages of
Jell-O made in one year would
stretch three-fifths of the way
around the globe.
Immigrants at Ellis Island were
served Jell-O to say "welcome to
America."
Andy Griffith eats Jell-O.
A bowl of wiggly Jell-O has brain
waves that are about the same as
grown-ups'.

Astronaut Shannon Lucid kept
track of time on Mir space station
by wearing pink socks and eating
Jell-O every Sunday.

Things to put in Jell-O
    Fruit cocktail with
        cherries
    Mini marshmallows
    Yogurt
    Anything that floats
    A note to your sister!

Things NOT to put in Jell-O
    Grapes (they sink)
    Grapefruit (it stinks)
    Ice cubes (they melt)
    Gummy worms (you can't
        see them)
    Barbie shoes (my Mom
        really did that once!)

Alex

Time: Present day
Setting: Alex's bedroom
Characters: Three sisters
Alex onstage. Takes a bow. Lights
come up.

Alex: (picks up shampoo bottle) This will be
the microphone. Whoever wants to talk has to
use the shampoo bottle.

Stevie: Says who?

Alex: Says me. Why? Because I'm oldest. That
makes me the director!

Alex: (to audience) Good evening, ladies and
gentlemen. Welcome to Alex's room, where two
sisters who do not live in this room (but think
they do) are always hanging about.

Joey: You called us in here for an SCM!

Stevie: Yeah, you told us it was The Sisters
Club.

Alex: Allow me to introduce myself. I am
Alex the actress, star of the Reel family. That's
Reel, as in film, or fishing. Not R-E-A-L as in
unreal. I am, for real, the F-O-B-S: First,

53

Oldest, and Best (Reel) Sister!

(Stevie throws a pillow at Alex. Joey throws a slipper.)

Please refrain from throwing rotten fruit and other objects such as pillows and slippers at the actors.

(Stevie takes the shampoo bottle.)

Stevie: I have a question. How come you get to go first when we have The Sisters Club?

Alex: First is best!

Stevie: You're conceited.

Alex: Confident. (Alex takes shampoo bottle back.)

Alex: Tonight's drama is a mystery. I have called you here to help me solve "The Mystery of the Missing Glitter." As the drama unfolds, we'll round up the usual suspects and discover WHO is the culprit. Who stole the glitter nail polish from big sister Alex's room?

Joey: (pointing to Stevie) She did.

Stevie: (pointing to Joey) She did.

Alex: I see we have a stalemate. Let's call in Sherlock Holmes. (Alex puts on houndstooth cap with earflaps. She holds out a crayon for a pipe. She props Sock Monkey up on a chair.)

Alex: (to Sock Monkey) My dear Watson, we must ask the suspects to hold out their hands. (Joey holds out hands. Stevie sits on hers.)

Alex: What's this I see, old chap?

Sock Monkey: I do believe we have caught BOTH suspects! (takes up Joey's hand)

Alex: Here I see minute traces of a highly reflective decorative material. Suspect Number Two has proven her guilt by concealing her hands altogether. Yes, Watson, I do believe the mystery is solved—in record time, at that.

Sock Monkey: What's the punishment?

Alex: The punishment, you say? The two shall hereby be banned from this room forever unless given written permission to enter.

Stevie: It was for science! I was helping Joey with constellations.

Alex: Is it not written in the stars that you shall never enter my room when I am not here?

(Stevie rolls her eyes. Joey jumps up and takes the shampoo bottle.)

Joey: How come you're like this now? You hardly ever play with us anymore. We never get to have any fun like we used to.

Alex: Hello! I'm twelve and three-quarters. I'm almost a teenager, not a baby.

Joey: Well, how come you won't let us touch your stuff anymore? Not just nail polish. Even your old Barbies you don't even play with anymore.

Alex: Reality check! They're M-I-N-E, just like this nail polish. Look at the evidence, right, Watson? (holds up Joey's hand)

Joey: What do you care, if it's baby stuff?

Alex: Grow up!

Joey: We used to always get to come in your room and have sleepovers and slumber parties and stuff for The Sisters Club. Remember?

Alex: I'm busy. I'm the oldest, don't forget. I have important things to do, like practice lines for my audition for <u>Beauty and the Beast</u>. I really want this part! Besides, as the oldest, I need my privacy.

Joey: What's privacy?

Alex: It means to be by myself. No sisters. Me, myself, and moi. I need to be alone.

Joey: Can't I help you be alone?

Stevie

I could not face eating a leftover pizza, Chinese takeout, or cornflakes for dinner one more time. Ever since Mom had gone back to work, we had not eaten together as a family—not once. Dad was busy building sets for Alex's play and directing a play next door at the Raven almost every evening. And once Alex caught play fever, that was the last we saw of her.

The closest we got to being a family was Joey and me eating dinner while we watched Mom on TV.

I decided it was time for me to step in and make an RFD—Real Family Dinner! (Reel Family Dinner!) I mean, how hard can it be to cook? But I wasn't about to do it all by myself.

First I tried to convince Alex. I even told her it was an emergency SCM. She said she'd be down in a few minutes (a.k.a. one hour!) after practicing her lines for the *Beauty and the Beast* audition, which she did like a million and one times a day.

I went to find Joey on Planet Jell-O (under the piano). She'd been living there all week, eating (what else?) lime Jell-O. It was all I'd seen her eat since Mom became Fondue Sue.

"Do you think pioneers ate Jell-O?" she asked me.

"No. Pioneers were smart. They knew if you ate too much lime Jell-O, your face and hands would turn green, and your ears would jiggle and fall off."

"Would not!"

"Would too! What are you doing under there, anyway?"

"I had to get inside my covered wagon because it was raining so hard."

"Well, it's stopped raining now. Come help me chop wood to start a cooking fire."

"But the wood's all wet. It won't light."

"C'mon, Joey! It's Family Dinner! Mom would not want us moping around feeling all sorry for ourselves."

Joey stuck her lip out.

"Stick out that lip any farther, and a chicken'll come lay an egg on it."

She pulled the lip in. I guess she did not want chickens roosting on her.

"Don't be stubborn. If I told you it's for homework, would you help?"

"Maybe."

"It's for homework."

"What kind of homework?"

"Science. Pretend we have to save something endangered."

"Like what?"

"Like we're saving the Family Dinner from going extinct around here."

"Can we make mac and cheese?"

"Sure, Duck. We can make whatever you want: sweet potato soufflé, crêpes suzette, jellied eel, roast rat—anything. Just not beef tornado."

Joey and I headed toward the kitchen, a Sisters Club of two. Joey sat at the table and wrote some more in her notebook. She wasn't exactly helping, but at least I had stopped her from living under the piano.

Names to call Stevie when she calls me Duck

Cheesy Mac
Bossy Betty Crocker
Betty Cracker
Sweet Potato Stevie
Soufflé Head
Crêpes Stevette

I opened the refrigerator. Three hairy peaches, green cheese, and an art project. "Hey! What are your constellations doing in the fridge?" I asked Joey.

"The glitter nail polish has to get hard."

"Duck! Go put this on the table."

Pout-face Joey put down her notebook and took her constellations to the (not-being-used) dining room table. I opened the butter door. "No butter, just film."

"Did you know Jell-O is really gooey stuff made from animal parts and they use it in film?" asked Joey.

"Gross! Well, we're not eating film, even if it is made of Jell-O! OK, forget about the butter. We'll use eggs, milk, and cheese."

"Green cheese? P. U.! We're going to eat green cheese?"

"We'll cut off the mold. Just like the pioneers!" Joey's face lit up when I said the magic word: "Pioneers."

She scribbled some more in her notebook.

I poured the noodles into the skillet and grated the cheese and beat the eggs and stirred the milk. All Joey did was play with the salt shaker.

"Joey! You're not helping. Here. Put two drops of hot sauce in."

"Whatever you say, Betty Cracker."

"I said two drops, not a flood! That stuff is really hot. Give it."

I stirred everything together. "Look. You turned the mac and cheese all orange."

"It doesn't look right anyway," Joey said.

She was right. The macaroni looked too small and burnt, not plump and fluffy like Dad's used to be in the good old days B.B. (Before *Beauty*). I'd seen Dad melt the cheese over macaroni in the skillet a hundred times. What had I done wrong?

"Where's Alex?" I asked.

"Not here," Joey said helpfully.

"Is she still practicing for tryouts? All she cares about is that play!"

"I know," said Joey. "Hey, let's make the whole dinner orange! We can have oranges and orange juice and stuff. Then they'll think we did it on purpose—like a theme!"

I wanted to like her idea. I wanted her to feel like she was a big help. "OK, we can have mac and cheese, and carrots and orange juice."

"And don't forget dessert," said Joey. "Orange Jell-O! Orange you glad I didn't say banana?"

"Oh brother," I sighed.

"Don't you mean sister?" she asked.

I spread a tablecloth on the living room floor. "Let's sit on the floor, Japanese style."

Joey was in charge of the (all-orange) centerpiece: a half-melted pumpkin candle, a snow globe of the Golden Gate Bridge (minus snow), a horn-toed lizard she got at the zoo, and socks.

"I hope they like orange dinners in Japan," Joey said.

Then everything started to happen all at once. Mom yelled, "I'm home!" Dad yelled, "What's that smell?"

Alex made an appearance (better late than

never!), peeking under pot lids and snitching carrots from the bowl. Some help.

Joey was running around collecting dirty pots and pans and putting them in the sink to soak. She squeezed like five million gallons of dishwashing liquid in there. I know she was trying to help, but honestly, it looked more like she was building an Eiffel Tower right in the kitchen sink.

I checked the table. Everything looked OK—pretty good, even—minus the mac and cheese, which looked super-strange, like astronaut food or something.

"Who made this?" asked Mom (minus any yummy noises).

"Crêpes Stevette," said Joey, not taking any credit for the orange mess.

"Um . . . why are there socks on the tablecloth?" Alex asked.

"Because they're orange," said Joey. "It's a theme!"

Everybody stared at their plates. I caught Joey doing the old napkin-under-the-table trick, feeding everything but the Jell-O to her napkin. Did she think I didn't know? I invented that trick.

"C'mon, you guys. It's not like it's *King Lear* jellied eel and rotten oranges." I tried to sound cheerful, but my own plate stared up at me, all orange and lumpy.

"*Bluck!* What is this?" I asked, pulling a particularly disgusting lump from my mac and cheese. "Ooh! It's an ear!" Gloppy cheese dropped from its lobe. "Jo-ey!" I couldn't believe I was the victim of the rubber ear trick—me, who invented that one, too!

Alex burst out laughing. "There's an ear in your macaroni? Yee-uck. I hope there aren't any elbows in mine." She poked it with a fork. "Or eyeballs."

Joey cracked up.

"Very funny, Duck," I said. "See how hard I'm laughing? Ha, ha, ha, ha, ha," I said, holding the cheesy ear out to her.

"I can't hear you," Joey said.

"Pass the salt," said Alex. "At least it's not orange."

"And it doesn't have ears!" said Joey,

cracking herself up all over again.

Dad was first to take a bite. *Crunch!*

Mom tried a mouthful. *Crr-unch!*

Alex swallowed. "Wa–ter," she gasped, holding her throat.

"What's wrong with everybody? This is supposed to be a Family Dinner," I told them. "You know, where we all get to be together, have conversation? Not just eat cereal from a box and watch Mom on TV."

Dad wiped his mouth about a hundred and one times with his napkin. Even Dad was using the old napkin trick!

"I'm not one to talk when it comes to cooking—" Mom started.

"I made it just like Dad!" I protested.

"Stevie, honey, you *did* boil the macaroni first, didn't you?" Dad asked. "Before you put it in the skillet?"

Joey looked at me and then burst out laughing, I mean really lost it this time.

"Carrots, anyone?" I asked, not even cracking a smile.

Alex

Mom: Stevie, Stevie, Stevie, you're so
wonderful, you're so great (for making a really
awful disgusting family dinner that made us all
want to throw up). Thank you so much, honey.
You're really a big help around here, blah blah
blah.

Alex: (mutters under her breath) What's
more important anyway—learning my lines so
I can be a STAR, or making some cheesy food?

Dad: OK, I guess I'm on kitchen patrol
tonight since I didn't have to cook. Who's with
me? Alex? Will you do me the honor of being my
Queen of the KP tonight?

Alex: (wishing Dad would stop acting like
I'm two) Dad! Stop sounding like the prince
asking Cinderella to a ball or something,
instead of asking me to wash greasy, grimy pots
and pans. It's really annoying.

Dad: (pinching my cheeks, which he knows
I hate) Can't a father do a little joking around
with his daughter anymore? C'mon, lighten up!

Alex: Dad, look, the dishes have to soak
anyway. It looks like Attack of the Orange

Blob in there. We should just put up a big sign, MACARONI DISASTER, and declare it an official disaster zone.

Joey: Hey! We could put up some yellow police tape.

Dad: Great idea. You know what your grandmother always said: "The best recipe—"

Joey and Alex: "—is eating out!"

Mom: It can't be any worse than the tuna noodle fiasco.

Stevie: Alex always gets out of doing chores and stuff. (to Alex) You said you'd help!

Alex: Hello? As if I have nothing better to do. You know I was busy practicing my lines for Beauty and the Beast.

Stevie: You mean for Beast.

Dad: Girls!

Mom: I thought I explained we're going to need a little cooperation around here, with me working full-time again.

Alex: I know, I know.

Mom: (Blah blah. . .tells some story about hard-boiling an egg. . .)

Stevie

Just when I thought Family Dinner couldn't get any worse, Alex said, "Hey, what's that sound?"

"Just the fridge gurgling," said Mom.

"Sometimes it does 'The Star-Spangled Banner,'" said Dad.

Everybody was laughing, except me. I wasn't laughing, because I saw something. Something moving, creeping down the hall right toward me, inching closer and closer.

Not a disgusting rat or giant termite or million-legged centipede or anything like that. It was a mountain of white, foamy, frothy SOAPSUDS, floating down the hall like a giant bubble bath coming at us.

"I'll be right back," I said, and raced for the kitchen.

That's when I screamed.

Alex and Joey came running, with Mom and Dad right behind.

Suds were pouring over the edge of the sink, slithering across the counter, sliding down the cabinets and across the floor, and swimming down the hall.

"Awesome!" Alex said, like she was admiring a work of art. "Which one of you hairy stinkpodes left the water on?"

"Don't just stand there!" I told her, as I pawed my way through piles of suds, miles of suds. "Turn off the water!"

"This is cool—like a car wash, without the car!" Alex said.

Joey yelled, "Giant bubbles! Whee!!" She picked up a handful of suds and blew on it. Bubbles flew through the air and landed on Alex's head.

"Not the hair!" Alex said. "OK, you're in for it now, Little Sister!"

"Look out! Attack of Mr. Bubble!" Joey screamed in a food-fight voice, and pushed some more suds toward Alex.

"Take that!" Alex said as she flicked some suds at Joey and me.

"Hey! You flicked me!" I yelled. "That does it." I grabbed a clump of suds in each hand and flung them at Alex.

She grabbed two handfuls of suds and flung them back at me, like a snowball fight.

Before I knew it, I was smack-dab in the middle of a giant bubble bath with my sisters! It was the most fun we'd had in weeks.

"Ooh, I feel some sliding down my back," said Alex.

"So? I got some up my nose. See?" said Joey.

Dad couldn't stand to watch. He had to get in on the action. He made himself a bubble beard à la Abe Lincoln and started reciting the Gettysburg Address. "Four score and seven years ago . . ."

While Dad was imitating one of our forefathers, Mom was standing there with her mouth open. All of a sudden I realized she might not think it's so funny.

I felt kind of bad for Joey. I knew she was just trying to help with dishes when she poured five million gallons of soap into the sink. She must have left the water running. I didn't want her to feel bad and get in trouble and go live under the piano again.

"I guess I left the water running or something," I blurted, covering for Joey. Joey stopped throwing suds. She stared at me.

"I see that," Mom said. Joey stared at Mom.

"Mom, I'm sorry," I said. "It's all my fault. Don't be mad. I'll clean it up."

"I'm not mad, honey," Mom said. "I was just thinking. Our kitchen probably hasn't been this clean since Hepzibiah McNutty herself lived here!"

Family Dinner
by Joey Reel

First you need a family.
Think of a theme (like the color orange).
Sit at the table together (even if it's on the floor).
Say "Pass the carrots" and "How was school today?"
The stuff you can't eat, put in your napkin.
Use only a TEENY TINY BIT of soap to do the dishes!
Family Dinner is kind of like a science project. It takes a lot of work and makes a big mess. You never know how it will turn out.
Family Dinner means everybody being together. It's way, WAY better than eating just Jell-O all by yourself.

Family Dinner makes you not want to live under the piano.

In the end, your stomach hurts. Not because the food was so bad, not because you ate a lot of orange stuff, but because you end up laughing so hard.

A+ for Family Dinner!

INTERMISSION

Stevie

Joey and Alex thought Family Dinner was a crack-up and a half, but I would have been wrinkled to a prune from cleaning up all by myself if Mom and Dad hadn't been there. Why is it that older sisters have too many other "responsibilities" to help, and younger sisters don't have any? I feel like the only, lonely member of The Sisters Club.

Being in the middle is like being invisible.

Think about it. The middle of a story is not the beginning or the end. The middle of a train is not the caboose or the engine.

The middle of a play is the intermission. The middle of "Monkey in the Middle" is a monkey. The middle of Neapolitan ice cream is . . . vanilla.

"I'm vanilla!" I shouted to anybody who would listen. *Plain old boring vanilla.*

Nobody.

Alex ignored me. She just kept writing stuff in the margins of her play script (what else is new!) and mouthing the words.

Easy for her. She's strawberry.

So I blurted it out. I told my family how I hate being the middle. Middle, middle, middle.

"Hey! The middle of 'Farmer in the Dell' is the cheese!" Joey reminded me.

"The cheese stands alone," I reminded her back.

Heigh-ho the Dairy-o, we all pound the cheese.

"And gets pounded," I added.

Alex looked up. "There's a book about that, you know. *I Am the Cheese.*"

Yeah. My autobiography, I thought.

"Wait. You think you're cheese or something?" Joey asked.

I ignored her. They just don't get it. I mean, the middle of a year is, what, Flag Day? The middle of a life is a midlife crisis!

I told my dad I was having a midlife crisis.

"You're going to give me a midlife crisis if you don't get over this," Dad said. "Life is not a dress rehearsal, you know! It's the real thing, and sometimes you only get one chance, but you can't go around taking it all so seriously."

That's my dad. Usually I like him fine, but I can't stand when he says cornball stuff like that. So I asked him to name me one middle that is a good thing.

Dad had to think. He thought and thought and didn't say a thing. Then finally he told me, "The middle of an apple is the core."

"Uh-huh. The yucky part people throw away," I said.

"How about the middle of the night? That's an interesting time, when people see things differently."

I pointed out that most people sleep through the middle of the night.

Then he shouted like he had a super-brainy Einstein idea. "The middle of an Oreo cookie is the sweet, creamy best part. You can't argue with that."

He was right. I couldn't argue. If I had to be a middle, that's the best vanilla to be.

"See? You're the peanut butter in the

sandwich," says Dad. "You're the creamy center of the cookie that holds it all together. You're the glue."

I'm the glue?

I'm the glue!

Glue is important, right? Glue holds the stamp to the letter, the pages to the book, the sole to the shoe. If I'm the glue, then I guess it's up to me to keep this family from falling apart.

ACT THREE

Stevie

It's a hard job, being the glue. Sometimes a person just doesn't feel very glue-y.

After the Macaroni Disaster, second only to Suds-O-Rama, I was more than ready to get back to school on Monday. Even the cafeteria's food was starting to sound good.

Only one problem. I had nothing to wear.

"Nothing to wear," I said out loud to my closet.

I was standing flamingo-style (on one foot) in my jeans and favorite flannel pajama top (covered with forks and toasters and fried eggs), staring at a bunch of hangers.

Joey wrinkled her nose at me. "You're starting to sound like A-l-e-x."

"And you sound like M-o-m."

I stared at the hangers some more. "You just don't understand, Little Sister." Joey wrinkled her nose again. "Stop wrinkling," I told her. "You look like a rhinoceros."

I went down the hall to Alex's room. I could hear her downstairs banging away on the piano. Only Alex would play Mozart at seven o'clock in the morning.

"You'd better not go in there without asking!" Joey warned. "Alex said!"

I went in anyway.

Joey stood with her toes just outside the doorway, so technically she did not step into Alex's room. "It's your life!" she told me.

I had another idea, a much better idea. I headed straight for the laundry room where I could hear the *whump, whump* of the dryer.

Perfect!

I opened up the dryer and took out Alex's soft, fuzzy red chenille sweater with the big pink star—her favorite. I used to have the same sweater in green, but I washed it with the red one and it came out looking like spaghetti in a blender.

Sometimes I know I'm being mean, but I just can't stop myself. A part of me knew Alex was dying to wear that sweater today, but the mean part of me didn't care. The mean part of me was sick of being in the middle, sick of being the peacemaker, sick of being invisible. I guess you could say it was one of those times I just didn't feel very glue-y. In fact, I felt just the opposite.

I yanked the sweater from the dryer. Perfect! All cozy-warm and soft as kitten fur, with an apple-clean smell. I put it on. The pink star grinned up at me.

For once, I would be the star, not Alex. I hurried and covered it up with my coat before anybody could see. I grabbed my backpack and ran down the street to Olivia's house, hoping to catch a ride.

I tried not to think about Alex or what would happen after school when I got home or anything. Nothing mattered except for that moment. What a great morning. And it was going to be a great day.

I, middle sister Stevie, had the power of the sweater.

During Language Arts, Ms. Carter-Dunne gave us ten minutes to pick a famous poem in our book. "I want everyone to choose a poem you like, then use it as a model to write one of your own. Look at the poem's style. Think about how it's written. Let the poem inspire you."

I flipped back and forth through the pages as fast as I could.

"This is an in-class assignment, people. I'll give you time to write, then we'll read some of them out loud."

Out loud, a.k.a. in front of the whole class! I broke out in a sweat just thinking about it.

I flipped some more. First I saw a Russian poem, but it had the word "breast." No way was I going to say "breast" in front of a bunch of fifth-grade boys. I almost picked a haiku about trees, but nobody gets a good grade for a haiku. It's only three lines!

Olivia picked "We Real Cool" right off the bat.

"No fair!" I told her. "What if I want that one?"

"Pick this one." She opened up a page and pointed.

"No way. The guy says he feels like an eggplant." That's when I saw the plums. Plums had to be better than eggplant! So I picked a poem by the plum-not-eggplant guy, a Mr. William Carlos Williams.

This Is Just to Say

I have eaten
the plums
that were in
the icebox

and which
you were probably
saving
for breakfast

Forgive me
they were delicious
so sweet
and so cold

I read it over a bazillion times. Then it hit me, like Mr. William Famous Williams himself was talking to me, Stevie Reel. He might have been talking about plums, but he knew just how I felt. About the sweater.

After we had quiet time to write our poems (with Ms. Carter-Dunne looking over our shoulders half the time!), she asked me to read my poem aloud in front of the whole class. *My poem.*

Why did she have to pick me? I tried to tell her it was private. I tried to tell her it really wasn't meant to be read aloud (to a bunch of immature fifth graders!).

I tried to tell her, but she said, "Oh, Stevie. Your poem is a perfect example for the rest of the class. It's inspiring! It's just what I'm looking for. No need to be shy."

Easy for her to say. Why do teachers think that telling you not to be shy will make you not shy? Guess what, Ms. Carter-Dunne, Queen of Reading-Aloud Poems— it just makes it worse!

I'm Sorry
by Stevie Reel

I have taken
your sweater
that was in
the dryer

and which,
you were probably
going to wear
today

Forgive me
I spilt chocolate on it
it wasn't fair
I used to have the same one

But, I still enjoyed
how everyone said
I looked better in it than you

So I, Stevie Reel, who hates acting (despite being a direct descendant of Hepzibiah McNutty), who hates standing up in front of people, had to stand in front of the whole class with sweat circles under my arms (in Alex's sweater!) and read my poem to twenty-nine pairs of squinty eyes (that's fifty-eight eyes!) while trying not to spit or spray or choke on the last line, or turn ten shades of red, or pass out from embarrassment.

At least I didn't have to say "breast!"

Stevie's Haiku

Why not a haiku?
Haiku's not embarrassing...
O for the haiku!

Joey's Homework Notebook

I wanted to do some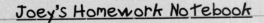
fifth-grade homework,
like Stevie. So I snooped in her
school folder. I found a poem she
wrote. (She copied some famous
guy!)

In third grade, Mr. B. won't let
us copy. When I asked Stevie, she
said:

#1) I'd better stop snooping in
her stuff.

#2) She didn't copy anybody. She
just got inspired (by plums?).

#3) I'd better not show Alex.
(I'm going to, of course!)

My poem is about sisters (NOT
sweaters!). Only I didn't copy any
famous guy. And I didn't get
inspired by plums.

Sisters Are Forever
by Joey Reel

Sisters copy.
Sisters talk to Sock Monkeys!
Sisters steal stuff and don't ask.
Sisters fight.
Sisters call you Jell-O names.
What goes away but always
comes back?
Sisters!

Alex

Alex: I had my audition today, Sock Monkey, for the best part ever: Beauty, in <u>Beauty and the Beast</u>.

Sock Monkey: Well, I didn't think you were the Beast!

Alex: Thank you! That's why I love you so much. Mww! Mww! (kissing sounds)

Sock Monkey: Then what's wrong?

Alex: I so did not get the part.

Sock Monkey: What do you mean?

Alex: First of all, I didn't have my lucky sweater.

Sock Monkey: How come?

Alex: Because my evil, wicked, un-stepsister Stevie stole it from the dryer.

Sock Monkey: That's evil! Wicked! Very step-sistery of her.

Alex: I know. But that's not even the worst part.

Sock Monkey: Oh no. What's the worst part?

Alex: I messed up my lines.

Sock Monkey: Everybody makes mistakes.

Alex: Not like this!

Sock Monkey: It can't be all that bad.

Alex: It is. Or as Beauty would say, "'Tis a sorrow, 'tis a tragedy."

Sock Monkey: What happened?

Alex: OK, see, there's this guy I like. His name is Scott Howell. He's in Drama Club, and he's really good at acting, and I know he's going to get the part of Beast.

Sock Monkey: So you want to star in the play with him, right?

Alex: More than anything. Maybe he could like me if we get to practice together and everything.

Sock Monkey: You can do it!

Alex: But wait, I haven't told you the bad part.

Sock Monkey: Go on.

Alex: We were practicing reading our parts and I kept noticing this zit he had on his face.

Sock Monkey: Gross!

Alex: I tried not to look at it. . .

Sock Monkey: Maybe he didn't see you see it!

Alex: I wish! That's not it. We were saying

our lines back and forth for the audition, and I was going along fine. It's the part where Beauty is trapped at her father's house, and she has a dream that Beast is dying. She wakes up and has a revelation.

The line goes, "I am indeed quite wicked to cause so much grief to Beast, who has shown me nothing but kindness. Is it his fault that he is so ugly, and has so few wits?"

Sock Monkey: What's wrong with that?

Alex: I messed up! Now I'll never get the part, and Scott Howell will hate me forever. Here's what I said. No lie. I said, "Is it his fault that he is so ugly, and has so few zits?"

Ha ha ha ha ha! (laughter from offstage)

Stevie

Yep, that was us. We, the evil, wicked un-stepsisters were eavesdropping!

Alex flung open the door. She glared at us with mice eyes, all puffy like she had been crying. She started swearing at us in Shakespeare. "You gor-bellied, hasty-witted harpies!" she yelled.

"Don't you mean hasty-*zitted* harpies?" I said, cracking up even more.

"How long have you been out there? You guys heard every word I said, didn't you?"

"Scott Towel has zits!" said Joey. She lost it, giggling like it was the funniest thing ever.

Joey's giggling egged me on. "Oh, Sock Monkey, I love you," I imitated her. "You're just an old sock, but you look just like my boyfriend, Scott Towel! Kiss kiss kiss."

"*Howell!* It's Scott *Howell!* If you're going to eavesdrop, get it right."

For once, we knew to keep quiet.

"And don't think I forgot you stole my lucky sweater! Where is it? I mean it, Stevie.

You'd better give it back this minute!"

"She can't," Joey said, cracking up some more. I covered her mouth with my hand.

"YOU!" said Alex. "You're a dankish elf-skinned clot-pode, no better than Stevie! If Mom were here, I'd—"

"I am not an elf or whatever!" said Joey.

"I hope you both turn to stone, just like Beauty's evil sisters in the fairy tale! I'd like you much better as statues, that's for sure!"

Joey looked at me as if she didn't know whether to laugh or cry.

"Out, vile jelly!" Alex shouted.

She slammed the door in our faces without waiting to get her sweater back. Thonk! The door slamming knocked a picture off the wall, a picture of Alex when she was the mushroom in *Mushroom in the Rain* in her kindergarten play. I wonder if she heard the thud from inside her room.

"You're still a mushroom!" I shouted, only because it sounded good. Silence. Was she still listening?

"Nothing short of a miracle will turn a

wicked and envious heart!" she shouted
through the door, quoting her beloved
Beauty.

Giggling. We were actually giggling
like crazy! And for some strange reason, we
couldn't stop.

"Sisters make me crazy, you know!"
yelled Alex.

"Ditto!" I yelled back.

"Double ditto!" yelled Joey, even though
she doesn't know what it means.

We both sat on Joey's bed (after moving
about a hundred stuffed animals), staring at
the mess that used to be Alex's sweater.

"Stevie?" Joey asked.

"Not now, Duck. I have to think."

"About what?"

"What to do about Alex, the sweater—
everything."

"She was calling us evil Jell-O and stuff!"

"It's Shakespeare. She always spits out
Shakespeare when she's mad."

"She doesn't even know you wrecked the
sweater yet. She just thinks you stole it."

"Don't tell, Duck! She's going to kill me when she finds out," I said. "Or at the very least, turn me into a zitty-faced stinkard!"

"She'll see." Joey pointed to the mess of yarn on my bed that used to be Alex's sweater. "It looks like a bird's nest. What happened?"

"I told you. The tag was itching me, so I cut it off. I do it all the time on my own stuff. When I washed it to get out the chocolate, the next thing I knew the whole thing came undone," I said.

"Maybe we could sew it," Joey suggested. "Mom could help us."

"How? She's not even here."

"Maybe we could make it into something else."

"What? Like a Sweater Monkey?" We burst out laughing all over again.

"Like a scarf, or a pillow for her room."

"Hey, that's a great idea, Duck. I think I can make a pillow, with the star on the front. At least she'd have something."

All afternoon, I tried to make a sweater pillow for Alex. It looked more like a bed for

Sock Monkey. It didn't help that Joey kept bugging me. "Duck," I told her, "go work on some made-up homework."

Finally, when I finished my not-a-pillow creation, I held it up for Joey to see. "I don't know, Joey," I said. "Maybe I should just never tell Alex—"

"Never tell Alex what?" said Sock Monkey (a.k.a. Alex) from the doorway. I hid the thing under my pillow.

"Nothing," I said as Alex came into the room.

"I'm not blind, you know. Something happened to my sweater. You lost it, didn't you? Or you left it at school and somebody stole it. Which is it?"

"I made you something," I said, sounding lame. I took it out from under my pillow.

"A *potholder?*" said Alex. "You made me a potholder?" She said "potholder" like it was a bad word or something.

"I was trying to make a pillow, but . . ."

"This is all that's left of the sweater—my lucky sweater? I had to audition for Beauty without it, and now I probably didn't get the part, all because of you." Alex ran down the hall to her room, clutching Sock Monkey. She slammed the door again.

"Do you think I should go talk to her?" I asked Joey.

"Nope," Joey said.

I tiptoed down the hall anyway. I knocked on Alex's door. Lately I'd been talking more to doors than to my sister.

"I know you're upset," I said to the door. No answer.

"Alex, c'mon, don't be mad. I'm sorry. I didn't mean to ruin your sweater. All I did was cut out the tag—honest—and it came all apart. What can I do?"

The door cracked open in the middle of my speech. Sock Monkey poked his button eyes through the crack. "You owe Alex one sweater. You'd better go buy her a new one. And she is not kidding. She means it," Sock Monkey said. All I could see of Alex were her teeth, smiling sweetly through the door crack, like she was acting for a toothpaste commercial or something.

"You've got to be joking," I told her. "I don't have money. That sweater cost like thirty dollars. Where am I going to get thirty dollars?"

"You figure it out," Sock Monkey squeaked. The door closed, not with a slam this time, but with a quiet click. It felt creepy—worse than a slam. Two seconds later the door opened and she hung a thingy on the doorknob that said, "Sister-Free Zone."

The door clicked shut again.

"Wait!" I said to the door. Only a slab of dark wood separated us, but it felt like the Great Wall of China. I put my ear to the door and tried to listen to see if she was still standing there, if I heard breathing.

All I heard was the door.

"You do NOT look better than me in that sweater!" said the door.

Thirty Dollars
by Joey Reel

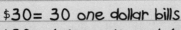

$30 = 30 one dollar bills
$30 = 1 twenty and 1 ten
$30 = 6 fives
$30 = 3000 pennies!

Ways for Stevie to get $30:
Wait till summer and make a lot
    of lemonade
Babysit cats or walk dogs
Rake leaves
Sell her hair like Jo in <u>Little Women</u>
Anything but find out about my
    money sock

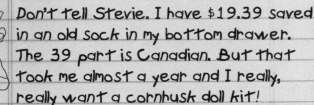

Don't tell Stevie. I have $19.39 saved
in an old sock in my bottom drawer.
The 39 part is Canadian. But that
took me almost a year and I really,
really want a cornhusk doll kit!

Alex

Time: After school

Setting: Standing in front of Drama Club bulletin board

Characters: Me (Alex) and Him (!)

Him: So, think you'll get the part of Beauty?

Me: (It's him. Beast! Scott Howell!) Oh, hi! (What a lame-o.)

Him: Hi. Alex, right?

Me again: (Don't say "zit," don't say "zit" . . .) I'm Alex. Reel. (He knows your name, Stupidhead!)

Him: I know. We read together yesterday at the audition, remember?

Me: Oh yeah. Sure. You're Scott Towel, right? (Wrong! I want to die ten thousand deaths right on this spot.)

Him: Actually, Scott Howell, with an H.

Me: (Blubber, blubber . . . say something. Anything!) Hamlet, put a knife through me now.

Him: Don't worry. I get that a lot.

Me: (choking) Excuse me?

Him: The paper towel thing.

Me: (First the zit, now this. He'll never speak to me again.) I'm sorry. It's just, see, my sisters—never mind. So! Have you acted a lot? (Better. Much better.)

Him: Ever since I played a pumpkin in my second-grade Thanksgiving play. (laughter here)

Me: Don't feel too bad. I was a mushroom in kindergarten! No joke.

Him: So, you're really into acting, huh? I hear your mom and dad act at the Raven and everything. Pretty cool.

Me: Acting is the greatest. It's like, I don't know, a chance to forget everything. Be somebody else. (Help! Do I sound intelligent or stupid?)

Him: So, what's wrong with being you, Alex Reel?

Me: No, it's not that . . . I just meant . . . Never mind.

Him: Is it like one minute you're you, this seventh grader with homework and parents and a little sister who bugs you—

106

Me: Two little sisters!

Him: (laughing)—and the next minute, you're saying stuff that was just words on a page a minute ago, but suddenly you believe it?

Me: Exactly! Wow! That's exactly it. The director calls "Curtain!" and there's a spot of light for you to stand in, and it's like you pick your character up off the floor and suddenly you're Anne Frank or Dorothy or . . .

Him: A mushroom?

Me: Yeah, I guess. (laughing)

Him: Well, I guess we won't know who got the parts till tomorrow, huh?

Me: You have to get Beast. You were so believable!

Him: Thanks, I think. It's a good thing to be good at being a big, ugly, hairy monster, right?

Me: Absolutely!

Him: Good luck.

Me: You too.

Him: See you tomorrow?

Stevie

Alex came home on top of cloud nine with flowers in her hair. No lie. She wore a braided crown of flowers (weeds, actually!) around her head *in public* on the bus home and at the library and at the grocery store.

If you haven't guessed already, Alex got the part of Beauty—even without her lucky sweater!

I was dying to point this out, but then again I was afraid to bring it up. I think, I hope, she's forgotten about the whole sweater incident because she's obsessed with:

A. Beauty (and the Beast)
B. Beauty (as in looks)
C. Paper Towel Man
D. Learning her lines (I'm supposed to help. Ha!)
E. Paper Towel Man (did I say that already?)

Paper Towel Man got the part of Beast.

Surprise, surprise.

He just called Alex on the phone. Joey answered and announced, "It's a boy!" for the whole world to hear, like a baby had just been born or something.

Alex didn't even get mad. (If I did that, she'd kill me!) She is over the moon. She showed Joey and me his school picture. This Scott Towel was about as big as a pinhead, so what was I supposed to say?

Joey said he looked just like a praying mantis! Ha!

OK, so I'm not jumping-up-and-down, falling-over thrilled for Alex like Mom would be. Where's Mom when you need her?

All I know is, Mom'll make me help Alex with her lines, over and over and over. And in this house, plays always end up in a fight.

Alex says I just don't understand the beauty of acting. I guess she's right. If you ask me, acting makes you sweat. Acting makes you want to throw up. Acting makes you afraid to fall. Take it from me, the Human Piñata.

Biography of Alex Reel,
Famous Actress

Alex Reel is the firstborn child of the actress Susan Reel, who has acted for many years at the Raven, and former actor Richard Reel, whose famous roles include King Lear.

Alex has always been the light of their lives. Gifted since birth, Alex follows in the footsteps of generations of Reel actors to perform in such plays as <u>Mushroom in the Rain</u> and <u>The Fifth Grade Nerd</u> (she was not the nerd), as well as <u>Heidi</u> and <u>The Sound of Music</u>. Her current role of Beauty in <u>Beauty and the Beast</u> is thought to take her to new heights on the way to stardom in an already stellar acting career.

Alex's Stage Names:
Alexis
Cricket Seagull
Alexandra Love Reel
Julia Trulove
Topaz

Alex

(Knock, knock. Make fake knocking
noise by clicking tongue in doorway of
sisters' room.)

Alex: (to sisters) Sisters Club Meeting!
Sisters Club Meeting!

Stevie: Now?

Joey: In here?

Alex: Your room's bigger. C'mon, you guys.
You're always saying we don't get to have fun
anymore. This'll be fun, I promise!

Stevie: Like how?

Alex: Like we're going to put on a play.

Joey: Yay!

Stevie: That's not a real Sisters Club.
That's just a way to get us to help you practice
your lines.

Joey: Who cares? C'mon, Stevie.

Stevie: Can't you just practice with Scott
Towel? I don't feel like—

Alex: You owe me. Don't make me say
"potholder"!

Stevie: OK, OK!

Alex: Good. It's all settled, then. I, the most beautiful sister, get to be Beauty. I will also be the director, of course.

Joey: You always get to boss everybody!

Alex: It's my play. Stevie, you're Beast.

Stevie: I'm Beast? What do I do?

Alex: First of all, you can't just say lines. Get into the character. Feel what it's like to be Beast.

Stevie: Feel what it's like to be all hairy and ugly?

Alex: You know what I mean. Here, put a blanket around you. It will help you feel more Beast-y. Joey, you're narrator.

Joey: Can't I be Chip the Teacup, like in the video?

Alex: You're going to be Joey the Broken Cup if you don't stop arguing. You're our stand-in if we need a tree or a horse, too.

Joey: A tree and a horse don't even talk!

Alex: Then do sound effects. OK, everybody, quiet on the set! Joey, start reading here. Action!

Joey: Once there was a merchant who was

very rich. He had three daughters. The youngest
was not only prettier than her sisters, but the
nicest.

Stevie: Hey! You're making that up.

Joey: Na-uh! Look. It says right here.

Alex: Okay, blah blah. Let's say all Beauty
asked for was a rose. When the dad picks one of
Beast's roses, Beast says the father must die
unless he gives him his daughter.

Joey: Hey! You just took my whole part!

Alex: Never mind that. Let's take up where
Beauty first comes to stay with Beast. Stevie,
upstage left.

Stevie: Huh?

Alex: It's blocking. Forget it. Just stand
over by the window. (Joey starts tapping yogurt
containers against desk for horse galloping.)

Stevie: Tell me now, do you not consider me
very ugly?

Alex: I do, since I cannot but speak the
truth. But I also find you very kind.

Stevie: Alas, in addition to being ugly, I'm
afraid I'm also dim-witted. I am a mere beast.

Alex: Say it like you mean it! And don't just

look out the window. Mr. Cannon says, "Respond to your fellow actors."

Stevie: Is Mr. Cannon this mean?

Alex: Stand like this, with your legs bent. Arm out. Mr. Cannon says, "Keep your character in your head, but let your body tell the story."

Stevie: Does Mr. Cannon say this play should be called <u>Blabbermouth and the Beast</u>?

Alex: (not listening) Nonsense. A dim-witted person would not admit it so. Besides, you have a kind heart. When I think of that, you are no longer ugly.

Stevie: Beauty, will you be my wife? (laughing)

Alex: C'mon, Stevie. You can't just crack up.

Joey: Oh, Beauty, my Beauty. Kiss me, O beauteous one. You know you want to. Mww, mww, mww. (makes kissing sounds) I'm not really an ugly Beast. I'm Scott Towel. Mww, mww.

Alex: Joey! We don't need sound effects for kissing!

Stevie: Hey, just so you know, I'm not going to kiss you or anything, if that's what you think.

Alex: Stop acting like babies, you guys. This is acting.

Stevie: I'm still not kissing you.

Joey: Here, kiss this! (shows roll of paper towels)

Stevie: Great idea, Joey. Paper towels can be Beast.

Joey: The paper towels can be Scott Towel. Get it?

Alex: I'm not kissing some roll of paper towels.

Stevie: Go with it, Alex. Feel the part.

Joey: Maybe this'll help. (draws face on paper towels)

Stevie: Perfect! (holds paper-towel Beast out toward Beauty) Beauty, will you be my wife?

Alex: No, Beast. I cannot.

Stevie: I know I am terrible, but I love you so very much. Promise me you will never leave me.

Alex: If you let me return to my father for eight days, I promise I shall come back to stay forever.

Stevie: Very well. But before you take leave, you must kiss me. Seal the promise.

Alex: (kisses paper towels) Mww! Mww!

Good-bye, Dear Beast. I shall miss you so.

Stevie: I can't believe you actually did it!

Joey: (ha ha ha ha ha) Alex kissed paper towels!

Alex: You guys have paper towels on the brain. Rule number one in acting is "don't be afraid to look stupid."

Stevie: You sure got that rule down. (Stevie and Joey fall on the floor laughing.)

Alex: You guys don't know anything—about acting OR boys OR kissing.

Joey: We know one thing. Alex is in love with a paper towel!! (falls on floor laughing some more)

Scott Howell Scott Howell Scott Howell Scott Howell Scott Howell Scott Howell Scott Howell Scott Howell Scott Howell Sco

Volcanoes
by Joey Reel

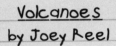

I woke up to a volcano in the living room!

Dad is pretending <u>Beauty and the Beast</u> takes place right here in Oregon! So there's going to be a volcano in the play, and I get to help make it.

I have to rip up about a million newspapers for the papier-mâché. My hands turn all black and stick together from all the gluey stuff. There are going to be layers and layers and they will take forever to dry.

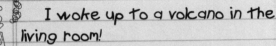

At least ripping up newspapers is better than acting—no kissing!

118

Things okay to kiss:
    Dad
    Hedgie
    School paper that gets an A+

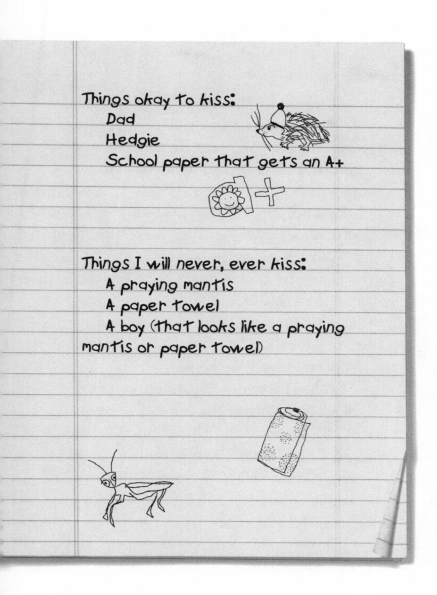

Things I will never, ever kiss:
    A praying mantis
    A paper towel
    A boy (that looks like a praying
mantis or paper towel)

Stevie

Alex put on The Hat at Family Dinner one night. Family Dinner (Tacos a la Stevie, minus any ears) was actually edible now.

"OK, I have something to say—an important announcement."

"Sounds serious," said Dad, tapping his spoon on a glass to get everybody's attention.

"What is it?" asked Mom.

"The play is only one week away, and we still don't know our lines. So I asked Scott, the guy who plays Beast, to come over and practice with me."

"Scott Towel?" asked Joey.

"Puh! That's your big announcement?" I asked, like *who cares*.

"Wait," said Alex. "There's more. I want to ask him if he can stay for dinner . . . but Joey and Stevie have to promise they won't embarrass me. I mean it. No calling him Scott Towel and stuff."

"Dinner? This does sound serious," said Dad, and he winked.

"I promise!" said Joey.

"I don't!" I said.

"First of all, Joey, and everybody, he is NOT my boyfriend. Second of all, if you embarrass me, I promise you will end up like the sisters in *Beauty and the Beast*—turned to stone!" She gave us an evil squinty-eyed look. "Not you, Mom and Dad—Joey and Stevie."

"Does this mean I don't have to be Beast anymore?" I asked. "If I have to say 'I'll die of hunger without your beauty' once more, I think I'll throw up."

"Hmm. I'll have to think of something special to make," Mom said.

"You mean you're going to be here?" asked Alex. "I mean, what about the show? I mean, you're hardly ever home in time for dinner."

"You want Stevie to cook, don't you?" Mom asked.

Alex nodded. It made me feel like I was appreciated, for once.

"I'll think of something," I said.

"You can make anything but Macaroni Disaster," said Alex.

"OK, but it'll cost you."

"Beast!" said Alex, just like old times.

Everybody tried to act normal, like Alex was just having a friend over, no big deal. But really you could tell everybody was holding their breath for the big night, all because it was A BOY.

I don't get what the big deal is about boys. I mean, they have huge feet and their ears stick out. They snort in class and call girls names like Maggot and Pootney. It's not like some prince was coming to dinner. (Well, maybe the FROG prince.) After all, the kid was a Beast.

I thought about trying to make something special. Really I did. After all, I still felt kind of bad about the sweater potholder.

Then I had a brainstorm, a brilliant, boy-coming-to-dinner brainstorm.

I saw it on Mom's show. Fondue Sue did

a whole show on fondue—the dinner you melt in a pot! You get these long forks and dip stuff like bread or strawberries into cheese or chocolate. It even has funny names like Chocolate Cherry Fun-due.

When I said I was making fondue, Dad starting having a major fondue flashback and telling 1970s stories about him and Mom bonding over melted cheese in a pot. He helped me find our fondue pots in the garage. So what if they were a little spidery. What Alex doesn't know won't hurt her.

Fondue was perfect for the big dinner:

It's French. (Alex would be all over that.)

How hard could it be to melt stuff?

If you drop fondue in the pot, something funny happens! (I can't wait to tell Joey!)

Rules for Boys Coming to Dinner:

Do:

Remember NOT to call him Scott Towel (right!)

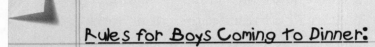

Set the table with paper towels for napkins

Wear nice clothes (Pioneer dress?)

Bump Scott to make his fondue fall off the fork!

Don't:

Bring up Sock Monkey

Show baby pictures of Alex

Let Dad tell embarrassing stories about the old days

Use the word "boyfriend" (unless you want to turn into a statue)

Q: Who is Scott Towel's brother?
A: Scott Tissue (a.k.a. toilet paper!)

Q: Who is Scott Towel's cousin?
A: Scotch Tape!

Alex

Alex: (enters with The Boy, looks at all the bowls on the table) Wait! Stevie? What's this? We're having croutons for dinner? (Not another Macaroni Disaster!)

Joey: Not just croutons. There's cheese glop, too.

Stevie: <u>Fondue</u>. It's French.

Alex: French? Of course! We're eating French tonight. Yum! French cheese glop.

Scott: Should I sit . . . where?

Stevie and Joey: (at same time) THERE! Next to Alex.

Joey: And me!

Dad: Fondue is French for "to melt."

Joey: I thought it was French for "to kiss."

(I try to turn Joey to stone with my thought waves.)

Mom: (trying to save the day) Mmm. Look at this creamy cheese and bubbly tomato sauce and chocolate for dessert. Where did you learn to make all this?

Stevie: Mo-om. I saw it on your show.

Alex: (to Scott) Um, my mom has a cooking show on TV.

Scott: Oh yeah. My mom said she watches you, Mrs. Reel. (Scott looks at Stevie.) So you made all this? Looks . . . interesting.

Stevie: Thanks a lot!

Mom: Stevie, why don't you tell Scott, and us, how this works?

Stevie: OK, you pick up one of these long forks. Then you get bread or a marshmallow or fruit, stab it with your fork, and dip it into one of the sauces.

Alex: What are they?

Stevie: There's cheese Fiesta Fondue and pizza fondue. This I call Chocolate Meltdown, and that one's Yin-Yang.

Joey: Yin-Yang?

Stevie: Chocolate and marshmallow.

Joey: Those aren't toe marshmallows, are they?

Alex: (Oh, no!) Joey, shhh! (Please please please don't let anybody ask what toe marshmallows are!)

Stevie: I made sure to use marshmallows

that Alex didn't put between her toes.

Alex: (Can't they keep quiet about any-thing?) (to Scott) Just ignore them.

Stevie: Eat the regular stuff first, like the bread and vegetables. Then you get non-toe marshmallows for dessert, or orange slices to dip in chocolate.

Alex: (with a glare) I hope that's the only orange thing tonight.

Joey: And guess what? (looks at Scott) If you drop your fondue, you have to kiss all the girls at the table!!

Alex: Joey! (What are those two up to? I'm going to kill them later!)

Scott: Um, she's not serious, is she?

Stevie: That's the rule!

Alex: You guys! (to Scott) Aren't little sisters really annoying?

Scott: (nodding) I know.

Joey: Does your sister call you Scott Towel?

Alex: JO-EY! (Alex Reel, promising young actress, found dead of embarrassment at the dinner table last evening . . .)

Joey: I didn't make it up, you know, about

dropping your fondue and kissing all the girls. Stevie learned it on Mom's show!

Mom: It's true. (Not Mom, too!) It's an honest-to-goodness custom that goes with eating fondue. Remember, honey?

Dad: Boy, do I.

Alex: Then you had me and lived happily ever after. OK, can we please talk about something else now?

Stevie: Does anybody need a paper towel— I mean napkin?

Mom: Why do we have paper towels for napkins? There should be blue napkins in the cupboard, Stevie.

(Joey and Stevie burst out laughing.)

Joey: I set the table. I really think we need paper towels. Good thing I put out paper towels for napkins, huh, Stevie? (Scott turns bright red.)

Alex: Jo-ey! (Boy, is she gonna hear from me later!) (to Scott) See what I mean? Sisters are the worst.

Scott: (covers mouth with hand and coughs)

Stevie: At least we don't go around kissing

paper towels, right, Joey?

Joey: And talking to a sock monkey like it's a person!

Alex: (OK, that's it. I'm gonna wrap my sisters up and send them airmail to the moon!) You guys! Mom, Dad, may they please be excused?

Joey: I'm not finished yet! I've only had one crouton. One crouton is not dinner.

Stevie: I made this whole dinner. I don't want to be excused.

Dad: Girls! How about . . . let's talk about the play. Have you two seen the rose garden I'm making for the outside of Beast's castle? Each rose is handcrafted out of tissue paper.

Alex: That's cool, Dad.

Dad: Scott, tell us about playing Beast. What's it like?

Joey: Are you going to be really, really hairy?

(Joey bumps Scott's arm for like the tenth time.)

Alex: JO-EY!

Stevie's Fascinating Fondue Facts

Fondue comes from the French word
  "fondre," which means "to melt."
Most popular fondue: cheese
Girl drops bread into fondue=kiss all
  boys at table
Boy drops bread=kiss all girls
Never drink cold water with
  fondue. You'll end up with a
  cheese ball in your stomach
  as hard as a rock!

Stevie's Pizza Fondue

1 pkg. Cheddar cut into cubes
2 cups shredded mozzarella
1 jar tomato sauce
1 loaf Italian bread for dipping

Mix cheeses and heat until melted.
Stir in tomato sauce until smooth. Dip
bread cubes into mixture.

Stevie

All during dinner, I kept looking at Alex who was looking at Scott Towel like she's all in love—like she actually *wanted* him to drop his fondue! I mean, what are the chances you'll actually marry the person whose name you write over and over one hundred times in your seventh-grade notebook?

Zero to none.

"Stevie," Alex asked, "are you actually going to eat that, or just hold it there for a year? You're causing a traffic jam, you know."

"I'm concentrating," I told her. (On not dropping my fondue, so I won't have to kiss anybody!) I carefully dipped my zucchini into the fondue pot. The plan was for Scott Towel to drop his fondue, NOT me.

Dad cracked one of his really bad jokes. "Honey," said Dad, in front of everybody, even The Boy! "I just want you to know, I'm so fon-due you!" Like "fond of"you. Get it? Ha ha ha. Dad must be from the planet Cardigan, like the sweaters Mr. Rogers wears.

We're talking old school.

Mom actually thought it was funny. Alex looked like she wanted to crawl under the table and disappear.

"Ee-uw! Dad! You made me dip my zucchini in chocolate!" I said.

Then The Boy spoke. "This is all good," he said.

"For melty, lumpy cheese glop, you mean," said Joey.

"This tastes much better than the fondue I made on TV," said Mom.

"Stevie, you're getting to be quite the cook," said Dad. "Good for you."

"Good for us," said Alex. Everybody laughed, even Mom.

I think they really liked the fondue. Even Alex said it was way better than Chinese takeout! I couldn't help it, though—I kept half-expecting to find a rubber ear à la Joey floating in the cheese glop.

I guess she was too busy with her bump-into-Scott routine. We planned it that Joey would sit next to Scott Towel. Even better, it turned out he was left-handed and Joey's right-handed. "Like normal people and NON-boys," Joey pointed out. So it was perfect for bumping elbows!

"If you're left-handed, it means you're creative," said Alex. "An artist."

"I think it just means you bump into stuff more," said Joey. "See?" She bumped Scott's elbow, trying to get him to drop his fondue off the fork.

After that, every time S.T. (Scott Towel, a.k.a. Scotch Tape) reached for the fondue, Joey went BUMP!

S.T. scooched his chair closer to Alex.

When Mom and Dad weren't looking, Joey bumped him again, and then played innocent. Still nothing happened.

S.T. gave Joey a cut-it-out look, but he didn't say it out loud. He just took a sip of water.

I tried to signal Joey, to make my eyes say, *It's not working! Do it again!*

That's when it happened!

S.T. had a hunk of bread on the end of

his fork. He dipped it into the cheese. He started to lift it out. He waited for a second while the cheese went drip, drip, drip, and just at that exact moment, I saw Joey go in for the kill.

BUMP!

His cheesy bread slipped and fell and landed—PLOP!—right smack-dab in the middle of the cheesy cheese.

I looked at Joey. Joey looked at me.

S. T. was still chasing his cheese lump around the pot, hoping he wouldn't get caught.

"LOOK!" shouted Joey, pointing to the lump in the pot.

"Empty fork!" I shouted. "Empty fork!"

"Uh-oh. Bad news," said Dad. "Looks to me like he dropped it."

"I didn't—really it was—she bumped me!" He pulled his fork out of the fondue pot and knocked over his glass of water.

"Sorry. I didn't mean to. . ."

"It's OK," Mom said, handing him paper towel napkins to sop up all the water.

"Alex first!" Joey shouted. "Kiss Alex first!"

S. T. turned tomato red, worse than pizza fondue. He pretended to wipe up some more water drips, and disappeared under the table. Nobody knew what to do. Alex looked like she was going to cry. Joey pushed back the tablecloth to see what he was doing under there.

Finally, Scott pulled his head out from under the table. On the way back up, he accidentally bumped into Joey's ear—with his lips!

Everybody was silent. Like the whole family got turned to stone.

"Bluck! Frog lips!" Joey yelled. She actually said "frog lips!" No lie. Then she got up from the table and ran to our room.

Without dessert.

I ran after her. No way was old Frog Lips going to plant a wet one on me. Gross!

<u>Bluck!</u>
by Joey Reel

B oys are blucky and yucky.
L eftie!
U cky, too.
C ooties!
K issed by a praying mantis!

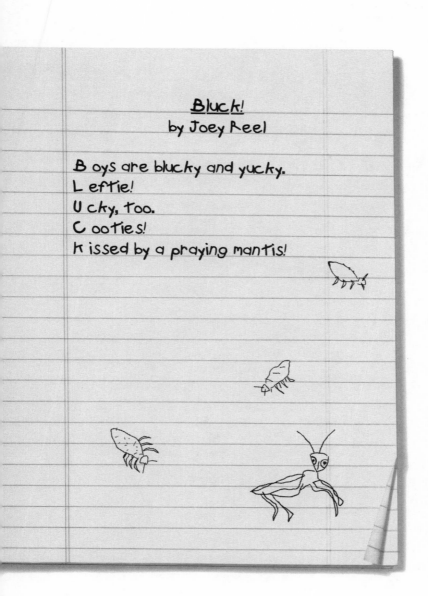

ACT FOUR

Stevie

"Open up!" I banged on the door to our room. "Hey, Joey! Let me in! Hurry up, before I get kissed by the Frog Prince!"

Joey opened the door.

"Phew, that was close," I said to Joey. She was already scribbling in that notebook of hers.

"Look what I'm making!" she said. She held up a NO KISSING sign—a pair of lips in a big red circle with a stripe through it.

"That's good!" I told her. "We can hang it on our doorknob like Alex is always doing."

Once Joey got over being kissed, we laughed ourselves silly just thinking about the look on S. T.'s face.

"Maybe I should draw an ear with a red line through it, too," Joey said. We cackled some more.

All of a sudden, we heard *Wham! Wham! Wham!* on the door. Definitely Alex. It was her you'd-better-open-the-door knock.

"Nobody's home!" Joey called.

"Let me in!" yelled Alex.

"Not by the hair of our chinny-chin-chins!" I called. That got Joey giggling all over again.

Alex burst in. "You guys are so not funny!" Alex said. "I asked you to be nice and you go and ruin everything, you—you—purple-hued maltworms!!"

"What did we do?" I asked innocently.

"You embarrassed me big-time in front of my friend and now he's left looking like he wet his pants 'cause you made him spill that water."

"Scott Towel wet his pants!" Joey said. I bit my cheeks to keep from laughing.

"And now Dad's taking him home and we didn't even get to practice the play or anything."

"At least you didn't have to practice kissing!" said Joey.

"I hate you!" said Alex. "I hate you both! I don't care what anybody says about sisters. I'm never speaking to you again. Ever."

"That's kind of hard when we live in the

same house," Joey pointed out. She was trying not to laugh.

"Oh, I'm so scared," I teased. "Like you could be quiet for more than two minutes!"

I knew Alex was mad—even madder because we were laughing—but I couldn't help teasing her. She looked so funny, with her eyes all on fire and her cheeks all puffed out and her face all squishy-mad. For some reason, I kept thinking of Dad's volcano in the living room. But I didn't know Volcano Alex was about to erupt—I mean *really* explode.

"I quit!" Alex shouted at us. "Do you hear me? I quit The Sisters Club! Forever and ever!"

Alex

Alex: I can't believe they'd do something like that! Can you?

Sock Monkey: Who? What?

Alex: My sisters! I mean ex-sisters. They wanted to embarrass me in front of my friend.

Sock Monkey: The Boy?

Alex: Yes, The Boy. So what.

Sock Monkey: You really like him a lot, don't you?

Alex: Duh! They had it all planned and everything, even after I asked them not to. Now I'll never be able to face him again—and I have to! Dress rehearsals start tomorrow night!

Sock Monkey: Mean.

Alex: Cruel.

Sock Monkey: Evil.

Alex: I know. Just wait, though. They'll be sorry. I'm never talking to them again.

Sock Monkey: Ever?

Alex: Never. You'll see. They'll be all, "Alex, play the Remembering Game. Alex, let's have The Sisters Club," and I'll be all, "What

Sisters Club?" As of right this minute, they are officially no longer my sisters. They're fired!

Sock Monkey: The play's almost here. Who's going to help you practice your lines?

Alex: You!

Sock Monkey: Me? How?

Alex: I'll be Beauty, and I'll say, "With one thing, I must own, I am well pleased, and that is your kind heart." Then you'll say Beast's lines.

Sock Monkey: "I have a good heart, true enough, but I am a monster."

Alex: "There are many who make worse monsters than you. Like my sisters, who think only of themselves."

Sock Monkey: Is that really the line?

Alex: It could be! Sometimes in acting you have to ad-lib, you know.

Sock Monkey: What would Beast say?

Alex: It doesn't matter. He'll probably never speak to me again anyway after my sisters humiliated him and made him look like a total moron. He didn't even stay for dessert! And we were supposed to practice our scenes together.

Sock Monkey: Is that really what you're so upset about?

Alex: Yes! Well, no. Yes and no.

Sock Monkey: You can tell me. You've always told me your secrets, since forever.

Alex: I'm afraid to say it.

Sock Monkey: Nobody's here. You can trust me. Do tell.

Alex: OK, the truth is, I . . . I think maybe I wanted him to kiss me. There. I said it. Are you happy now?

Sock Monkey: The Boy?

Alex: Yes! The Boy! How many times do I have to tell you?

Sock Monkey: Why did you want The Boy to kiss you?

Alex: I don't know. Just to see what it's like, I guess. But then my ugly un-stepsisters ruined everything.

(Alex holds Sock Monkey up to the mirror)

Together: "And because of their wicked ways, the two shall not be spared. It is their fate to stand at the door of Beauty's palace, still as stone, witnessing all of life from afar."

Stevie

Since Alex wouldn't talk to me, I thought I'd listen in on her talking to Sock Monkey, as in "spy." I was lying on the floor (under the bed) where I could hear most of what she was saying through the old iron grate where the heat comes through.

"Are you living under the bed now?" asked Joey.

"Shhh! Can't you see I'm trying to eavesdrop?"

"On who?"

"Alex and Sock Monkey!"

"What are they saying?"

"Mostly just *Beauty and the Beast* stuff. Stuff about us, too!"

"What stuff?"

"The usual. Evil wicked stepsister stuff."

"She's really mad at us this time, huh?" said Joey.

"Volcano mad!" I said. "But at least volcanoes only erupt every two thousand years."

"What's wrong with her, anyway? Why's

she acting so funny like this?"

"Mom says maybe it's hormones. Dad says it's a midlife crisis, between being a kid and being a teenager. Maybe it's a mid-love crisis! I just heard her say she wanted Scott Towel to kiss her!"

"No way!"

"Way!"

"I wish she would talk to us," Joey said. "Do stuff like we used to."

"Me too, Duck."

"And stop thinking we're purple meal-worms."

"Purple-hued maltworms?"

"Whatever. Is she really quitting The Sisters Club, you think?" Joey asked.

"You can't quit your sisters, Duck. Sisters are forever. Remember?"

"I miss Alex, and The Sisters Club. I even miss her bossing us."

I didn't say anything. But the real truth, the whole truth, and nothing but was that I missed my sister, too. She could have been talking to me, whispering me secrets. Instead, she was spilling her guts to a stupid old sock monkey, telling it she wanted to get kissed. By a B-O-Y! I just didn't get it.

"Hello!? Earth to Stevie."

"I know, I know. You want to show me something."

I slid out from under the bed. Joey cracked up. "You should see you! You have dust bunnies all over your hair!"

"And I found a Lego fairy, two quarters, and the silver locket from your pioneer doll."

"Hey! I've been looking everywhere for those! And I lost two quarters."

"Did not!"

"Did too!"

I handed Joey the locket and the Lego and put the quarters in my pocket.

"Are you coming or not?"

"Not."

"C'mon, Stevie. Please? You have to."

I followed Joey downstairs. One sister mad at me was enough.

Joey had been helping Dad paint the volcano. She took me by the hand and led me around to the back of the volcano. "Look! Look what I did! It's so funny!"

I crouched down on my knees and saw where Joey had painted initials with a big red heart around them.

"Joey, are you nuts? That's not funny. Alex is mad enough at us already!"

Joey stuck out her pout-face lip. "Well, I think it's funny. Besides, who's going to see it? It's in the bottom corner."

"I'm telling you, you'd better paint over it if you ever want your big sister to speak to you again."

Sisters
by Joey Reel

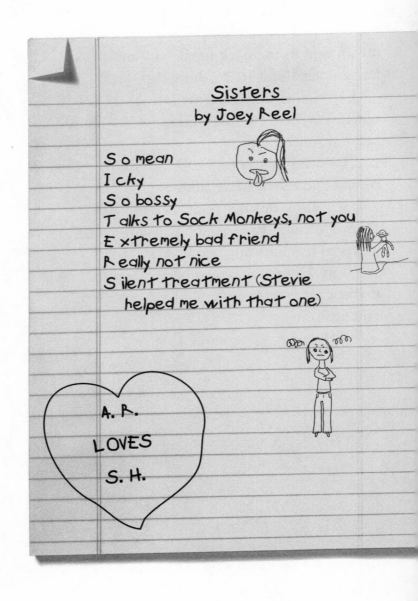

S o mean
I cky
S o bossy
T alks to Sock Monkeys, not you
E xtremely bad friend
R eally not nice
S ilent treatment (Stevie
  helped me with that one)

A. R.

LOVES

S. H.

Stevie

It felt terrible to be in a house full of silence. I'd been in Alex's House of Bad Moods before, but this was different, like a rubber band that you stretch too far and it snaps. Like a bowl you break by mistake, and it stares up at you in pieces.

Ever since Mom got her show and Alex got into the play, something had changed. Something sure felt broken, worse than a sweater that got wrecked or a dinner that went haywire.

Like our whole family was coming apart.

Take, for example, the night of Alex's dress rehearsal. Joey and I were downstairs checking out the volcano to see if it was dry.

"How's it look?" Dad asked.

"Well, a little lumpy," I said. "But the lava's really cool." Dad had rigged up an orangey-red light inside the volcano. It gave off an eerie glow.

"Volcanoes are supposed to be lumpy," Joey said.

"I thought we'd turn it on for the final scene," said Dad. "Very dramatic!"

"And look, this goes at the top for lava." Joey handed a bowl of cherry Jell-O to Dad and he set it on top of the volcano.

"Only you, Duck, would think of Jell-O for a volcano!"

"That looks awesome!" Alex said, coming into the room with her costume half on.

"Thanks!" said Joey.

"She speaks!" I said.

"I was talking to YOU, Dad, not the Traitor Sisters."

"I think we're just about ready for tonight," said Dad. "There's still a little wet paint, but it'll dry by the time we get to the school."

"Dad, you really outdid yourself," said Alex.

"I helped!" Joey said.

"Dad, will you please tell Joey to stop talking to me?"

"What?" asked Dad from behind the volcano.

"Never mind. Dad? Mom's not home yet.

Do you think you can help me with this costume? The sleeves are way too long. I feel like an octopus. Can you help me pin them up?"

"I don't want to get paint all over your costume," Dad said. "Stevie'll help you."

"Yeah, Stevie'll help you," I said. "All you have to do is ask her."

"Dad, will you tell Stevie I'm not going to ask her for help?"

"Why not?" asked Dad.

"Yeah, why not?" I asked.

"Dad, will you help or not?"

"Honey, I have a million things to get ready. We leave in forty-five minutes, and I have to load up the castle and the volcano—"

"They're not coming, too, are they?" Alex asked, pointing toward Joey and me. "Dad, can you please tell Stevie and Joey no way are they going to my dress rehearsal?"

"I'm going," said Joey. "I'm helping Dad with sets."

"And I don't want to stay by myself," I said.

"Mom'll be home. I mean, Dad, can you tell Stevie to just stay home?"

"We're all going, Alex," said Dad.

"Then please tell Joey if she's coming I'd better not hear a peep out of her tonight!"

"Peep," said Joey.

I decided it was up to me to fix it, make things right with Alex again. After all, I'm the middle sister. I'm the glue, right?

Middles are the peacemakers. I read it in a magazine once, a real magazine, not like the ones Alex is always making up and pretending she read somewhere.

Famous middle children:

George Washington

Harriet Tubman (I think!)

Madonna

Henry the VIII

Princess Di

Jan from The Brady Bunch

Martin Luther King, Jr.

HARRIET TUBMAN →

MADONNA →

GEORGE WASHINGTON →

HENRY the VIII →

JAN →

PRINCESS DI

MARTIN LUTHER KING JR.

I would have to pull a Martin Luther King, Jr. on my family. Only one problem—Alex still wasn't speaking to me. So I had to start by getting her to talk.

I waited till Saturday. I woke up early, before Joey or Alex. I went downstairs and made Alex her favorite breakfast. Then I carried it up to her room on a tray, like Mom used to do when we were sick.

I knocked on Alex's door. "Alex! Wake up!"

No answer.

"I made you breakfast," I said. "Your favorite!"

"Blueberry pancakes?" She spoke! It was a start.

"No."

"French toast with blueberries?"

"No."

"Blueberry anything?"

"Blueberry waffles!" I said. "With warmed-up maple syrup."

"Just leave it outside the door."

"I can't."

"Why not?"

"It's breakfast IN BED. It's no fair if you have to get out of bed."

"And who do you think's going to open the door? Sock Monkey?"

"C'mon, Alex. Let me in."

"But I'm not talking to you."

"You just did."

"That was a fluke."

Miracle of miracles, the door opened. Alex stuck Sock Monkey through the crack. She made Sock Monkey say, "You can bring Alex the breakfast, but that's all."

I pushed open the door.

"Alex, you can't stay mad at me forever, you know."

"Yes, she can," said Sock Monkey.

"But I can't stand it if you're mad at me for like the rest of my life. I can't stand it if you don't want to be my sister. C'mon, Alex. I've said I'm sorry like a million times."

"Alex said to tell you a million and one times is not enough for what you did," said Sock Monkey.

"Well, then, how can I make it up to you—I mean her? I mean . . . I made you breakfast. And I did the dishes for you, and I didn't tell Dad it was you who flooded the bathroom."

"Alex *so* did not flood the bathroom!" said Sock Monkey.

"Well, there was a lake on the floor, and Dad was mad, and Alex was the last one in there."

"Stop changing the subject," said Sock Monkey. "Alex is the one mad at you, remember?"

"How can I forget? You won't talk to us, and it's making Joey cry. Just tell me what to do—anything. I'll kiss Sock Monkey. See? Mww." I kissed that worn old bag of stuffing right on his ruby red sock lips. "I'll kiss paper towels if you want me to!"

Even Alex could not hold back a smile.

"Okay. I'll speak to you and Joey again," said Alex the person. "But that's all. This doesn't mean I'm your friend. This doesn't mean I'm back in The Sisters Club. It's not over, you know. You owe me. And you'd better make it up to me."

"How?"

"You'll think of something."

"Then you'll come back in the club?" I asked.

Cartoon by Stevie

Stevie

Opening night. That's the biggest night of the play.

Everybody was backstage buzzing around like bees, rushing around half-dressed and pacing back and forth holding scripts and mouthing lines to themselves. Mr. Cannon, the director, was racing around with a clipboard shouting orders to people. Actors kept coming up to him saying stuff like, "I can't find the rose for the rosebush" or "Am I supposed to come onstage before or after the word 'night?'" or "My hair won't stay on right."

Even I couldn't help catching a little of the excitement.

Joey was trying to make up for the frog lips incident, so she yelled, "Hi, Scott Towel!" to Scott, a.k.a. Beast, who was only half-hairy so far (from the neck down) and kept putting Listerine strips into his mouth.

Alex was talking a mile a minute. Every few seconds she'd stop and blow into her hand, taking a bunch of deep breaths. She sounded like a hyperventilating hyena. She looked like she was going to throw up on Dad's shoes.

Dad said, "Alex, honey, try to stay calm. Turn your nervousness into excitement. Remember your deep breathing? Now's the time. Breathe. Don't forget, if you blank on a line, or say the wrong words, just keep going."

"I know, Dad. The show must go on."

"That's my girl. I'll be backstage, checking on my scene changes, if you need me."

"You look beautiful, honey," Mom said, and gave Alex a non-frog-lips kiss.

"Mom! I don't even have the rest of my costume on yet. And you're messing up my stage makeup."

"OK, well, you still look beautiful."

"Dad, did you remember the moat around the castle?" Joey asked.

"It's all there, honey."

"And are you sure you got the volcano in the right place, facing the right way and everything?" It was just a hunk of cardboard and wire and paste, but you'd think Joey had helped build the Golden Gate Bridge or something.

"Five minutes!" Mr. Cannon called.

"Thank you, five!" the cast members called back.

Five minutes till show time. Time to go find our seats.

"Good luck!" I called to Alex.

Alex turned around with a mean glare. "Stevie, don't say that! Good luck is like bad luck in acting!"

"Whatever."

"Take it back!"

"OK, OK! I take it back."

"Break a leg!" Joey called.

The best part about plays is sitting in the dark. You have hundreds of people around you, but the dark makes it seem like it's just you, alone, you and the play. You get to laugh and cry and feel stuff and forget everything else, like homework, and fondue fiascoes, and sisters being mad at you.

Being in the audience is the best. You're inside the story, only you don't have to be up there acting.

Nervous. Shaky. Sweating.

Feeling like you're about to throw up.

If only Joey would stop whispering all the lines. I had to keep elbowing her, fondue-style. Once I even bumped her so hard I made her drop her Junior Mints.

Alex didn't seem one bit nervous. She didn't sound like a hyena anymore. Of course, you can't see the somersaults inside a person's stomach. They must be there. But she didn't even mess up one time in all of Act One.

Not even when I hunched down, crept down to the pit in front, and snapped a bunch of pictures of her.

Not even when the curtain got stuck.

Not even when Beast's nose fell off!

She did all the stuff Dad was always telling her—like when to look out at the audience and how to speak loud enough and all that junk. I don't know how she keeps it all in her head.

And she looked just like Beauty in the fairy tale. Not like someone who slams doors, throws herself facedown on her bed, and talks to a Sock Monkey. Not like someone who swears in Shakespeare or gives you the silent treatment or puts marshmallows between her toes.

I tried to think of myself in that dress, to imagine what it would be like. Picture it. It was a big step up from the Human Piñata, that's for sure. I wondered if the dress and the makeup help transform you, I mean, make you feel like you're somebody besides yourself.

I got so caught up in the story and the costumes and characters, the first act went by in a flash. Before I knew it, the curtain fell with a hush, and we could hear the patter of feet as the stagehands changed the scenery.

Alex

<u>Beauty and the Beast</u>, Act Two

Setting: The house of Beauty's father

Beauty: (bursts into tears) (Real tears!
This is good!)

Beauty's sister: Beauty? Whatever is wrong
that causes you to weep so?

Beauty: I've had a most frightful dream
this night. I was in the palace garden, and a
lady appeared to me. She showed me Beast, lying
on the grass, nearly dead. My poor, dear Beast!
I fear I've made a most dreadful mistake. (I
haven't forgotten one line so far!)

Sister: Nonsense. You belong here with us,
with Father.

Beauty: I fear I am indeed very wicked to
cause my poor, dear Beast so much grief. He has
shown me nothing but kindness. Why did I not
wish to marry him? (Act Two is almost over—
they love me!)

Sister: Marry him! Have you lost your senses?

Beauty: Is it his fault that he is so ugly,

and has so few wits? (Yes! I didn't say "zits!")

Sister: Perhaps not.

Beauty: Why did I not wish to marry him? It is neither good looks nor brains in a husband that make a woman happy. It is goodness, kindness, and beauty of character. (This is the best play ever! I'm a star!)

Sister: Certainly you would not be so foolish as to think yourself in love with a Beast?

Beauty: Yes, and to prove my love, I shall remove this ring. (I hope I can get it off!) Soon I shall find myself back at the palace of my beloved, where I belong.

Sister: NO!

Beauty: Alas! 'Tis too late, my dear sister. Good-bye! (I wish this scene wasn't over! Maybe if I ad-lib, add just a line . . .)

Beauty: (holding hand to head) Beast, O my dear, sweet Beast. Where art thou? (Run around stage—look here and there. Exit by the volcano. Oops!)

CRASH! (Audience gasps.)

Beauty: "Curtain! Curtain!"

Curtain falls on Act Two.

Crash!
by Joey Reel

Stevie

Just when I was starting to think maybe acting wasn't so bad after all.

When the houselights came up at intermission, Mom and Joey and I ran backstage to check on Alex. A girl came rushing up to us, the one who plays one of Beauty's sisters in the play.

"Mrs. Reel—you gotta come—now," she said, all out of breath. "Alex! Her foot—it's bad—all swelled up like a baseball."

Mom pushed through the crowd and ran up the stage steps, with Joey and me right behind her.

Alex was propped up against a wall, her leg sticking out. Dad was holding an ice pack to her ankle. Mr. Cannon and a bunch of the cast were all around her. Her makeup was all runny and her dress looked like a deflated birthday-party balloon.

Everybody was talking. In the blur, I heard "sprain" and "twisted" and "broken."

I heard Alex say she couldn't get up.

She couldn't stand or put any weight on her foot.

"What happened?" I asked, squeezing through the crowd.

"Didn't you see? Everybody else in the whole world did," Alex said.

"I know. But how?"

"Somebody painted AR + SH in a big red heart on Dad's volcano. I saw it right before the show, so I got some of the stage crew to help me turn it around a little. But I forgot that corner was sticking out, and I fell."

I was thinking, *See! I told you acting makes you fall!* but I didn't say it.

I knew she was going to say the play was ruined. I knew she was going to say it was all my fault.

"I didn't do it!" I said.

"We know, honey." Dad pulled Joey over close to him. He must have known she painted those initials on the volcano.

Alex didn't get mad. She didn't say it was all my fault, or Joey's. She started to cry.

"I've worked so hard for this, and now—"

"Maybe you can still go out there," I said.

"Yeah, right! I can't even stand up."

Alex looked so pathetic. I wished there was something I could do.

Mr. Cannon was pacing back and forth with his clipboard. "Think, people. We have to think. What are we going to do? We still have Act Three to go. It's short, but it's the most important act, the grand finale."

"Alex, are you sure you can't go out there?" somebody asked.

"I don't know . . ."

"You have to tell us now if you really can't go out there, honey," said Dad. "We've only got a few minutes."

"She's not going anywhere," said Mom, "but the hospital. We've got to get that foot checked."

"Mom, please. I'll be okay," Alex said. "Just till after the play. It's almost over. C'mon, you guys. It's opening night." She said it like it was her wedding or something.

"Couldn't we just wrap her foot up or

something, so she can walk?" I asked.

"There might be a fracture," said Mom. "It's already swollen. We can't let her put any pressure on it. She has to prop up her foot, and keep that thing iced."

"Okay, Alex," said Mr. Cannon. "If you can't, you can't. I don't want you to hurt yourself more than you already have. We'll think of something."

I was trying my best to think of a way to be helpful. "Don't you have an understudy?" I asked. "Somebody who knows all the lines, and could take Alex's place? Act Three's really short. There's hardly any words!"

"Janeena. She's the understudy," said Mr. Cannon. "But she's sick tonight. Maybe we can just go out and explain to folks what happened."

"It's Opening Night!" said Alex. "You can't just tell everybody to go home. People will be mad. And want their money back or something. If I know anything about acting it's that you don't quit. You keep going, no matter what!"

"But nobody knows the lines," said Mr. Cannon.

"I see before me a prince, more beautiful than Love itself," I quoted. "But where is my Beast? What has become of him?"

"Stevie!" said Alex. "That's it! It's perfect! Mr. Cannon," she called, "my sister Stevie knows all the lines. We've practiced this scene at home like a million gazillion times." She turned to me. "You mean—really—you would do this for me?"

I must have been crazy. Loony. I don't know what got into me. Me! The only Reel without an acting gene! Suddenly, I didn't think I could go through with it.

I thought of telling Alex I'd gone nuts. Temporary insanity. I thought of saying I didn't know the lines. I thought of running out the back door.

But then I looked at my sister. She looked like a raccoon, with her stage makeup all smeary. I looked at Mom. She nodded yes. I looked at Dad. "You know what I always say. The show must go on!" Dad said.

"Where's the dressing room?" I asked.

"Act Three cast members," called Mr. Cannon, "four minutes and counting."

"Thank you, four," everybody called back. Including me—Beauty.

On my way to get dressed, Alex and Joey hooked pinkies with me and we said our secret chant, "Sisters, blisters, and tongue twisters."

Alex pressed a tiny gold star on a chain into my hand.

"What's this?" I asked.

"It's from my baby bracelet. I always wear it. Put it on."

Since good luck was bad luck in acting, I asked, "For bad luck?"

"Yes! Now go!" Alex whispered. Joey added a little push, and before I knew it, I was dressed and made up.

Guess what, everybody? The dress didn't help. The makeup didn't help. Not even the Sisters handshake and the bad luck charm seemed to help.

I did not feel like Beauty one bit. I felt

more like Scarecrow in *The Wizard of Oz*.

"Curtain time!"

My knees went all wobbly. I had not walked in high heels since I was four. My eyes kept sticking together from all the makeup, and my dress crackled as loud as a potato chip bag when I walked onstage.

Return of the Human Piñata.

In my head, I could hear Alex saying, "Try not to blink so much," and Dad saying, "Remember to say your T's at the ends of words" and "Walk like you have a book on your head," and Mom saying, "You'll be fine," and Joey saying, "Go kiss a paper towel," but I really wasn't hearing any of them.

Then the curtain went up. The room got spooky quiet. It was so dark, I couldn't see any faces out there.

I pretended it was *King Lear*.

At home.

In my own living room.

I took three deep breaths (Dad would be proud) and walked right out onto that stage. (With a little push from Joey. But, hey, what are sisters for, right?)

A light shone on Beast like a moon-beam. He was lying down in the garden. I was supposed to come up on him from behind the volcano and think he was dead.

The light was so spooky and everything was so quiet, I almost believed it myself.

I stepped into the story.

"Where, O where, is Beast? Why hasn't he come?" I said, looking around. Then, when I saw him there, like he was really dead, I threw myself down, landing on my knees, and bent over him.

He smelled funny, like Tic Tacs and old attics.

I almost lost it. I could hardly keep from cracking up. I bent down to pretend I was listening to his heartbeat.

"My dear Beet! Your heart still beasts!" I said. Oh no! I was supposed to say, "My dear *Beast*. Your heart still *beats*." I was getting all tongue twisty. Why did we say "tongue twisters" right before I came onstage?

I said the line again. I think I sprayed

him with spit that time.

Scott Towel, from deep inside his hairy costume, whispered "Water" without moving his lips, and I remembered this was the part where Beauty was supposed to go get water from the canal.

When I came back, I threw the water in his face.

That part was fun! Way better than spit.

"Beauty! Is it indeed you? You forgot your promise! The grief I felt at losing you made me wish to die of hunger. Now I must die, but not without the pleasure of seeing you once more."

He sat up. I kept trying really hard not to think of paper towels.

"Dear Beast, you shall not die," I said. "You shall live and become my husband. Here and now I offer you my hand, and swear that I shall marry none but you."

The stage went pitch-black. Scott threw off his Beast head. He unzipped his hairy costume to reveal the Prince costume underneath. Lights blinked and flashed all around us. Music blared. A trumpet sounded.

Then I said, "I see before me a prince, more beautiful than Love itself. But where is my Beast? What has become of him?"

Scott Towel explained about the wicked fairy, and how she had put a spell on him, turning him into a Beast, until someone agreed to love and marry him.

All of a sudden, while Scott was giving his speech, I remembered.

Help! It was coming.

The moment Alex had waited for.

The kiss!

I'd forgotten all about it. I'd been so busy thinking of Alex, and the one thing I could do to make her want to be my sister again.

I couldn't look at Scott Towel. I stared at the floor.

I couldn't think. I didn't know what to do. Alex would kill me if I kissed him. But she'd kill me if I didn't, too.

Just pretend he's a roll of paper towels, I told myself. *Paper towels, paper towels. . .*

And before I knew it, Beast kissed me—

my cheek, anyway. I turned my head to the side in the nick of time.

The audience went wild. I guess it was OK. Alex wasn't going to kill me after all.

Once I got through the kiss, the rest of the play was a blur. I was standing here, standing there, stage left, stage right, saying this, saying that. It was like I was floating. All the words came out. I didn't throw up once. For ten minutes, I felt like a princess. And here was Beast, telling me I was to become his queen.

He took my hand and we walked through the doorway of the castle.

"As for your sisters," said the lady from Beauty's dream, "they shall be turned to stone. Their statues will stand at the gates of your palace."

She tapped each sister on the head and they froze in place, like in the game of Statues we used to play in the yard.

She told the sisters, "Only when you recognize your faults can you return to your former state."

"That may be a long time indeed," I said,

adding a line that wasn't in the script. The audience roared.

"Nothing short of a miracle will turn a wicked and envious heart," said the lady.

You know the rest—the happily ever after part and all that.

There you have it.

The curtain fell. The audience clapped for a long time. Alex used one of the play props, an old umbrella, to hobble out at the end and take a bow. She got a standing ovation, and I got to take two curtain calls with her! I know the clapping was mostly for Alex, but a part of it was for me, too.

Alex even gave me flowers. (The ones she sent to herself!) She kept the ones Mom and Dad gave her.

Dad used to say to me, "You're a member of the Reel family. You'd better start acting like it." I know it's corny, but that's Dad.

I guess I'm a real member of the Reel family after all.

Stevie

Can I just say, Broken-foot Alex is much nicer than regular Alex!

The week after the play, Alex sent us a note (not a silent treatment note—a real invitation, in writing, with glitter!) that said:

WHO: Stevie and Joey
WHAT: Special (not emergency!) Meeting of The Sisters Club
WHEN: Tonight, Friday the 10th
WHERE: Alex's room
WHY: Surprise!
Be there! BYOSB!

I guess she couldn't help bossing on that last line. But the rest of it was so cool, especially the part about Bring Your Own Sleeping Bag.

"She UN-quit!" said Joey. "Alex is back in The Sisters Club!" She was spinning. That's Joey—human merry-go-round. (She spins in circles sometimes when she's happy—don't ask me why.)

I had some surprises of my own in mind, too!

Sisters, blisters, and tongue twisters!

When we got to Alex's room that night, it was dark, but the ceiling shone with glow-in-the-dark stars. Candles, real candles, flickered all around the room. It was like stepping into a magical scene from *The Twelve Dancing Princesses*.

"We don't have to put on another play, do we?" I asked.

"No, Princess Smarty Pants," said Alex. "Just sister fun!"

"Yippee!" said Joey. "Are we sleeping over? For real?"

"For real!" said Alex.

"A sleepover!" said Joey. "Under the stars, just like pioneers! Can we eat funny food and have a pillow fight and tell fortunes and scary stories and play the Remembering Game and stuff?"

"Whatever you want, Duck. This is your night. Our night. Just us sisters."

First, Alex gave us each a pillowcase with our name on it, so we could each have our own pillow for the pillow fight.

"You actually sewed these for us, as in embroidered?" I asked.

"Who knew?" said Alex.

"Wow!" said Joey. "This is good. My favorite color, too."

"All colors are your favorite, Duck," I told her, and we cracked up.

"Well, Mom helped," said Alex.

"Mom?" asked Joey.

"Our Mom? The one who stirs her coffee with a pencil?" I asked. "And makes spaghetti in a blender?"

"Just because she can't cook doesn't mean she can't do other stuff like sew. She made Joey's pioneer dress, don't forget."

"OK. I have something, too," I said. "From Joey and me. We hope you like it."

Alex opened the box. It was a new fuzzy sweater, but instead of a star in the middle, it had the word BRAT.

"It's almost just like my lucky sweater! I LOVE it." Alex put it on over her PJ's.

"Are you sure? 'Cause I couldn't find the one with the star."

"It's really cool. Thanks, you guys!"

"Dad helped us!" said Joey.

"Really?" asked Alex. "Dad hates going to the mall."

"He said it wouldn't kill him to see how the other half lives—whatever that means," said Joey.

"Whatever you do, don't cut the tag out," I told her. "And DO NOT let me wash it— ever. Unless you like that spaghetti-in-a-blender look."

We played Chaos and Yahtzee and Boggle and, best of all, the Remembering Game. Joey remembered the Macaroni Disaster, I remembered Suds-O-Rama, and Alex remembered when I was Beauty in the play. It made me feel good that she knew how hard it was for me to get up there in front of the whole world.

I think it was her way of thanking me.

We painted each other's toenails with glitter nail polish. (Alex actually let us use her stuff without doing a Sherlock Holmes on us!) I took a picture of our three feet, something to remember this night by.

Then we ate Baked Alaska (three Klondike bars Alex hid under a cake pan lid) and (my surprise) Triscuits.

Pizza Triscuits and Mexican Triscuits and Triscuits a la Stevie (melty cheese and olives). Triscuits with ketchup, Triscuits with tuna fish, Triscuits with whipped cream and strawberries. Even make-your-own Triscuits.

"These are yum!" said Joey.

"What's with Triscuit mania?" asked Alex.

"I'm thinking of entering a contest,"
I said. "For the most original Triscuit recipe.
You can win like a million dollars or a college
scholarship."

For dessert, we toasted marshmallows by
candlelight.

Joey got out a fondue fork, put three
marshmallows on it, and held it up to the
candle. "Just like camp!" said Joey. "And this
is the campfire."

"This is great! How'd you ever think of
this?" I asked Alex.

"I read it in a magazine," she said.

"What, like the *Marshmallow Times?*"
I asked.

"Kidding!" she said, and we all died
laughing, remembering marshmallow toes.

"If this is the campfire, we have to have a
spooky story," said Joey.

" 'The Three Sisters!' " Joey and I yelled
at the same time. "The Three Sisters" is our
favorite story. Alex tells it the best, because
she always changes it around to keep us
guessing.

"C'mon, Alex! Tell it! Tell it!" Joey said.

Then I took up the chant. "Tell it! Tell it! Tell it!"

"OK, OK," Alex said. "You don't have to get so hyper. I'll tell it!"

Alex

Alex: Once a long time ago there were three sisters—

Joey: Just like us?

Alex: Just like us. All three sisters were going to be married.

Joey: Even me?

Alex: Even you, Duck.

Joey: I hope his name was Reginald.

Stevie: Reginald sounds like a dope! I hope his name was anything but Paper Towel!

Alex: Do you guys want to hear the story, or do you want to keep interrupting?

Joey: Story.

Stevie: Interrupting.

Alex: They had to travel a long way in their wagons. It was scary, and lonely, and dangerous. All the time they were crossing rivers and traversing mountain passes.

Joey: What's traversing?

Stevie: Shhh.

Alex: But it was worth it, all the loneliness and hardship were worth it, because at the end

of their journey, each would be reunited with
her true love.

Stevie: (sarcastically) How sweet.

Joey: Shhh! This is getting good.

Stevie: Just 'cause you're gaga for pioneers.

Alex: You guys! OK, so the story goes, one
dark night they arrived at the inn where they
were to meet their true loves, who were to have
come down out of the mountains that day. But
something happened—something terrible.
Nobody showed up.

Joey: Nobody?

Stevie: Not even one out of three?

Alex: Shh. Listen. Nobody showed up and
the three sisters were brokenhearted. They
wept all night. One was certain her love had
been killed in a blinding snowstorm. Another
thought hers had drowned in a mountain lake,
and the third was convinced that her love had
been buried in an avalanche.

They wept and wept until . . .

. . . the next day. Finally, they hiked to the
foot of the mountain. They made a crude marker
out of wood, so each sister could carve the

name of her true love. The oldest sister went
first.

Stevie: Of course!

Alex: The oldest sister carved the name of
her true love. The other two sisters, when they
saw it, fainted. All of their true loves were one
and the same!

Joey: They all loved the same guy?

Alex: Yes, but he had disappeared. They
never ever saw him again.

Stevie: What a creep.

Alex: Don't you mean "what a stinkard"?

Stevie: A pox on him for sure!

Joey: What happened then?

Alex: Years later, after the sisters died,
there was a terrible earthquake that split the
mountain into four mountains. To this very day,
they call the mountains the Three Sisters.

Joey: You said four.

Alex: Three are together. One is off in the
distance—Mount Bachelor. But nobody could
live near the Three Sisters.

Joey: Why not?

Alex: The mountains are volcanoes. Every

two thousand years they erupt, because the
sisters are still so angry at the guy.

Joey: Why couldn't they still live there the
rest of the time?

Alex: Oh. Well, because of the moaning.
Oooooo, aahhhhhh. The chilling sound could
always be heard whistling and moaning through
the mountain passes, and it haunted the people
of the village of Acton below. Some said it was
just the wind. Others were certain it was the
three sisters, moaning for their lost love.

Joey: Really?

Alex: Some got so frightened, they moved
away. But no matter how many villagers came
and went, the Three Sisters stayed together
forever, for the rest of time.

Joey: You gave me shivers.

Stevie: Me too.

Alex: So be it. That is the legend of the
Three Sisters. Just look out the window.

(The three sisters climb on Alex's bed and
kneel, looking out the window.)

Stevie: There's a full moon! Hey! I think I
can see the Three Sisters!

Joey: Listen! I think I hear something, like moaning!

Stevie: That's a cat.

Alex: Look at all the shadows. I love full moon nights. They make you feel all different and quivery.

Stevie: I know.

Alex: Did you know all the full moons have names, like Moon of the Raspberries and Wolf Moon and stuff? Tonight is called the Full Long Night Moon.

Stevie: That's cool. Did you read that in a magazine?

Alex: No, a calendar.

Joey: Let's make this the longest night ever.

Stevie: Duck, it's way past your bedtime. You can hardly keep your eyes open now.

Alex: Before we go to sleep, we have one more thing to do.

Joey: What?

Alex: Make a wish.

Stevie

Alex reached and pulled something out from under her bed. It looked like a tiny stack of origami paper tied with a pink bow.

"What is it?" asked Joey.

"Wishing paper," said Alex.

The paper was wispy-thin, like you could almost see through it. On the front were gold and birds and red stamps of Chinese characters.

"We each get one," said Alex. "You have to make a wish, then throw it in the fire. So let's each make a list of wishes first, like a rough draft. Then pick the one you really, really want. We can take turns burning our wishing papers in the candle."

"Did you ask Mom if we're allowed to do this?" I asked.

"Yes, but we have to do it over a cookie sheet. I promised."

"Do we have to say 'Sisters, blisters, and tongue twisters?'" Joey asked.

"Yep. That's a good idea, Duck. Then our wishes will go into the universe and come back true."

"Can the wish be a dream?" Joey asked.

"It can be a dream," Alex said.

Joey gave us each a slip of paper to write practice wishes on.

<u>Stevie's dreams (and schemes!):</u>

World peace (family peace, too)
My own room
Publish a poem
WinTriscuit contest
or start my own business
Always have The Sisters Club

Alex's hopes, dreams and plans for the future:

Be on Mom's show
Get S.H. to sign my cast
Never eat another Triscuit
Play Juliet someday

Joey's Wishes:

A million dollars
Pioneer camp
A baby sister
    (someone to boss!)
To hold a monkey
    (not a sock one)
To never EVER be kissed by a boy

$
5000
4000
1000
20000
1500
5000
16000
3000
50000
100 000
5000
1 000 000

After we sent our wishes out into the universe, Joey and I helped Alex blow out all the candles. I curled up into my sleeping bag, with my new Stevie pillowcase on my pillow. The room smelled all cinnamon-y, like it remembered having candles.

Before I fell asleep, I thought about my one tiny wish, floating out there in the wide, wide universe, under the Moon of the Longest Night. I imagined my wish floating right next to Alex's and Joey's, high up as a star. Maybe our wishes would make their own constellation, one that kids would point to on summer nights and say, "Hey, isn't that the Three Sisters?"

"I wish I was ten," Joey said to the dark.

"You're not supposed to say what you wished for!" said Alex.

"That wasn't my wish for the universe. I just thought of it right now."

"How come ten?" Alex asked.

"'Cause ten's the BEST age," I said.

"In *The Long Winter*, Laura Ingalls Wilder says—" Joey began.

"Here we go," I said.

"You read *The Long Winter*?" asked Alex. "*The Long Winter* is like the longest book in the world. Even I never finished it."

"Longer than Dad's all-time favorite, *War and Peace*?" I asked.

Joey cut in. "In *The Long Winter*, it says Baby Carrie was not really a sister until she was ten. When she turned ten, Laura said she was old enough to really be a sister."

"Go to sleep, Joey," said Alex.

"You're really a sister," I whispered to Joey before we fell asleep.

The only sounds now were the heartbeat tick of the clock, the hum and creak of house noises, Alex breathing.

I lay on the rug in the middle of my sisters, Alex on one side, Joey on the other, like perfect bookends. I couldn't think of anywhere I'd rather be.

In the middle. The best place to be.

FADE OUT